S0-EKK-629

THE FIDELIO AFFAIR

THE FIDELIO AFFAIR

Hilary Green

Chivers Press • Thorndike Press
Bath, England • Waterville, Maine USA

LP

This Large Print edition is published by Chivers Press, England, and by Thorndike Press, USA.

Published in 2002 in the U.K. by arrangement with the author.

Published in 2002 in the U.S. by arrangement with Hilary Green.

U.K. Hardcover ISBN 0–7540–7436–6 (Chivers Large Print)
U.K. Softcover   ISBN 0–7540–7437–4 (Camden Large Print)
U.S. Softcover   ISBN 0–7862–4505–0 (Nightingale Series Edition)

Copyright © Hilary Green 1985

All rights reserved.

All the characters and incidents in this book are entirely fictitious and no reference whatsoever is intended to any living person or actual event.

The text of this Large Print edition is unabridged.
Other aspects of the book may vary from the original edition.

Set in 16 pt. New Times Roman.

Printed in Great Britain on acid-free paper.

British Library Cataloguing in Publication Data available

Library of Congress Cataloging-in-Publication Data

Green, Hilary, 1937–
    The Fidelio affair / by Hilary Green.
        p.   cm.
    ISBN 0–7862–4505–0 (lg. print : sc : alk. paper)
    1. Terrorism—Prevention—Fiction. 2. England—Fiction.
3. Large type books. I. Title.
PR6057.R3425 F53 2002
823'.914—dc21   2002074332

East Bonner County Library
1407 Cedar Street
Sandpoint, Idaho 83864

203–1372

CHAPTER ONE

Nick Marriot folded his hands round the mug of coffee and watched the lights of the Pier Head pie stall reflected in the hurrying waters of the Mersey. A light breeze fingered its way inside the collar of his jacket and made him shiver. Although the May night was mild, three o'clock in the morning was a shivery sort of hour. He turned his head and looked towards the slope leading down to the landing-stage. With the tide ebbing the floating stage was out of sight, as was anybody who might be standing on it. He wondered how long Stone was likely to be and reflected with painful irony that he had no reason to hurry, bearing in mind the company he was in. If it had been him, he would have lingered over the meet as long as possible. For the hundredth time he resisted the temptation to walk over and look down.

The sound of the shot was so out of context with the picture in his imagination that it took him several milliseconds longer than it should have done to react. Then he was racing down the slope to the landing-stage. Only one figure stood by the edge of the water, slender, dressed in dark trousers and jacket, the lights from above striking a faint gleam from close-cropped blond hair and a darker, more metallic glint from the barrel of the automatic.

1

It was then that he registered that the sound of the shot had been followed by a splash. He skidded to a halt at the edge of the landing-stage. The dark water sluiced by below his feet, unbroken. He ran to the opposite side and looked over. No sign of form or movement disturbed the river's oily flow. Wild-eyed, he turned back to the girl who still stood with the gun in her hand. Behind him, the sound of a police siren wailed and died on a dispirited moan and feet thudded heavily on the ramp.

'Why?' he gasped, staring at her. 'Why?'

It was all he had time for before the two policemen were on them, disarming the girl, who made no attempt to resist, and bundling them both back towards the waiting car in spite of Nick's violent protests that they should be searching the river—that somewhere in those dark waters Stone might still be alive.

* * *

'Elizabeth Anne Walker, you are charged that at Liverpool in the County of Merseyside on the 29th May you did murder Peter John Stone. You are not obliged to say anything but anything you do say will be taken down in writing and may be given in evidence.'

The detective sergeant looked at the young woman in front of him. Beneath the close-cropped hair the face had a sculptured perfection and the huge, delphinium-blue eyes looked back at him unwaveringly. There was something unnerving about the combination of beauty and icy calm. For a moment it looked as if she was going to speak but then the lovely mouth twisted into a faint, ironic grin and she shook her head. The sergeant looked down at the papers on the desk in front of him; the collection of leaflets which they had found at the girl's lodging—each of them bearing the logo of a rising sun and the heading 'Daughters of the Sunrise' and dealing with subjects which varied from how to disrupt production in factories to how to foment street violence and racial hatred; the extra clips of ammunition for the automatic she had been carrying; and the signed statement admitting her guilt. He nodded to the constable and the WPC by the door.

'Take her down.'

In the Bridewell below the police station Nick heard the door of the cell next to his own open and slam shut. Sitting on the edge of the bed he sank his head onto his hands and stared at the wall which separated them. His stomach was sick and his brain numb with the effort of going over and over what had happened, trying to make sense of it; trying to come to terms with the fact that his partner and closest friend had been shot by the woman whom they both loved, and whom either of them would unhesitatingly have trusted with his life.

3

It had begun like any other mission with a call over his car radio. He had been on his way home after a frustrating trip down to Southampton to check on a man who had been picked up by immigration and who had turned out in the end to bear no resemblance to the suspect he was looking for.

'Delta Two, this is Control. Alpha wants to see you.'

Ten minutes later he was parking his car in the underground car park of the Spartacus Health Club, just off St Martin's Lane, noticing as he did so Stone's car already in the next slot. He called through to Control and then stepped into the special lift and inserted the plastic identity card which operated the mechanism to whisk him smoothly up past the swimming-pool and the squash courts, past the saunas and the gymnasia, to the top two floors which housed the offices of the Special Security Service; known to those who worked for it as Triple S but referred to by some outside of it, those who knew of its existence at all that is, as the Snake Pit. The lift carried him past the first of these two floors, where the control centre and communications room were situated, to the penthouse which provided both office and living accommodation for the organization's Head, James Pascoe—known to his subordinates, by logical extension, as Hissing Sid.

Stone was already with Pascoe. In fact, from

4

the relaxed atmosphere and the whisky glasses, Nick concluded that the official business had been completed. However, Pascoe came sharply to life, with an abruptness which helped to justify his nickname, as soon as Nick appeared.

'I've given Stone all the details so I won't waste time repeating them, since you both have to be in Liverpool tonight. You will travel separately, using the usual commercial rep cover, and check into the St George's Hotel, where you will meet accidentally in the bar and strike up an acquaintanceship. After dinner, at Stone's suggestion, you will have a night on the town.'

Nick glanced at his partner and grinned. The idea of a pub crawl at government expense was the sort of thing that would normally have appealed to his sense of humour, but to Nick's surprise there was no response. Stone's gaze was abstracted, as if he was only half listening.

Pascoe went on. 'You will finish up in the small hours at the Landfall Club, a converted destroyer down in the docks, and shortly before 3 a.m. you will head back towards your hotel. On the way you will stop at a coffee stall on the Pier Head. You, Marriot, will wait there while Stone keeps a rendezvous with a lady with whom you are both acquainted.' Pascoe leaned forward. 'I want it clearly understood that only Stone is actually to be present at the meeting. She clearly specified that there should not be more than one of you.'

Nick drew a deep breath and kept his eyes turned away from Stone. 'Very good, sir.' Then, after a moment, 'What is Leo involved in? I take it it is Leonora we're talking about.'

Pascoe rose. 'Stone can tell you all you need to know. Collect anything you need to support your cover from Control—and make it good. One more thing I want you both to have absolutely clear. This operation is strictly a YOYO.'

Nick grimaced. He understood the meaning of the acronym only too well, and it always gave him a feeling of insecurity. It meant 'if anything goes wrong You're On Your Own'. In other words, they could not break their cover even to ask for assistance from local police and if they ended up in trouble Pascoe would deny all knowledge of them.

'What happens after the meeting?' he asked.

'After?' said Pascoe, and paused fractionally. 'After, you can come back home again.'

'What's it all about?' Nick asked Stone as they went down in the lift.

'Pascoe didn't tell me much,' Stone replied. 'You know what he's like. He wouldn't tell the Archbishop of Canterbury what date Christmas is, if he could avoid it. Apparently Leo's in the middle of some undercover operation which involves posing as a member

6

of an extreme left-wing feminist organization called "The Daughters of Sunrise". She's got something to pass on which is highly sensitive and specified one of us.'

' "One" of us,' Nick repeated. 'Either one?'

Stone gave him a brief, lop-sided grin. 'I guess I just got lucky—for once.'

Nick pressed his hands over his face. Lucky! It had been light for some hours now. He had asked every time anyone came near him if they were searching the river—if there was any sign of a body. The answers had always been negative. He had stuck to his cover story when they questioned him, and had seen that they were surprised at the intensity of his anxiety over the fate of a casual acquaintance. He knew he must try to pull himself together but it was hard when his mind lurched so sickeningly from the thought of Stone's death to the memory of Leonora, standing there with her eyes wide and calm and the gun still smoking in her hand.

The door of the cell opened.

'The inspector wants to see you.'

He was taken up to an interview room. The DI behind the table got up as he came in and offered him a chair, then sent the constable for tea.

'I'm sorry we've had to keep you waiting so long Mr—Marriot. But you're free to leave any time now.'

Nick blinked. 'Any time?'

The DI nodded. 'The young woman has made a statement which makes it clear that you were not in any way involved. I'm sorry we had to inconvenience you, but I'm sure you can understand our position.'

Nick leaned forward. 'You mean she's confessed to the murder?'

'Yes.'

'Did she—did she say why she killed him?'

The DI lifted his shoulders. 'She's involved in some kind of revolutionary women's group, it seems. According to her statement, the man she shot was not an innocent commercial traveller but some kind of undercover agent for Special Branch or something. She maintains that he'd been hanging around for some time, trying to infiltrate the movement by striking up an affair with her.'

'Could that be true, do you think?' Nick asked ingenuously.

'No chance!' The DI laughed briefly. 'Everything we found in your friend's car and in his hotel room confirms that he was exactly what he told you he was—a rep for a firm of sports goods manufacturers. We phoned the firm and they confirm that he's been with them for nearly three years. What's more, he hasn't been in this area for six months.'

'Then why?' Nick repeated.

Once again the DI shrugged. 'Two possibilities, I suppose. Mistaken identity, perhaps. Maybe she thought he was some

8

other guy who had been hanging around, someone she thought was a plain-clothes copper . . .'

'Or . . . ?' Nick prompted.

'Or she's some kind of nutter. You say he took her for a prostitute. Perhaps she shot him because he propositioned her and then invented the rest.'

Nick stared at the carpet between his feet, remembering that calm, unnatural gaze. Was it possible that somehow, amid the conflicting strains of the different lives and personalities between which she was constantly moving, the central core which was the real Leonora had cracked? Had she begun to believe the fictions which she created with such conviction?

The constable came in with the tea. The DI said,

'Will you be staying in Liverpool?'

Nick shook his head. 'No. I'll go straight back to London—if that's all right with you.'

'As long as we have an address where we can contact you. You will be needed to give evidence, of course.'

Nick nodded, only half listening. 'You haven't—found the body yet?'

'No. The lifeboat is out now, searching, and we've got police divers checking the docks; but he went in on an ebb tide. The body might be washed up on Formby shore or somewhere, but it won't surprise me if we never find it.'

'There's no chance that he might not have

been killed—that he could have hauled himself out of the river somewhere?'

'If he had, someone would have found him by now, or he'd have got himself to a hospital or dialled three nines.' He looked at Nick sympathetically. 'I know it's tough when you come across this sort of thing for the first time, but I think we have to assume that Peter Stone is dead.'

Nick swallowed. 'What about his—his things? Can I—help, at all?'

The DI shook his head reassuringly. 'You can leave all that to us, Mr Marriot. We'll contact the next of kin and so forth.'

Nick rose and the DI came with him to the door.

'I should try to get some sleep before you think about driving back, if I were you. You look all in.'

Back at the hotel Nick showered and shaved and then went along the corridor to Stone's room. The door was open and a chamber-maid was making up the bed. Obviously the police had finished in there. The dressing-table was bare, the room empty except for the standard items provided by the hotel. Every trace of Stone's presence had been removed. Not that there would have been much, Nick reflected. Stone always travelled light. Even his flat in London looked more like a hotel room than a home—tidy, immaculate, uncluttered with personal mementoes or the normal bric-a-brac of everyday living. Nick's rooms, with their colourful muddle of posters and record sleeves and *objets trouvés*, used to annoy him intensely. He liked his living accommodation to be like his life; spare, ordered and stripped for action.

Well, Nick thought, as he drifted back to his own room, whoever had the job of packing his things wouldn't find it a long one—except for the contents of the wardrobe. It was there, if anywhere, in the row of expensively tailored suits and the leather jackets and cashmere sweaters that some hint of Stone as a person might linger. The police would have trouble tracing the next of kin he reflected, imagining them, with a trace of grim humour, following up all the carefully placed leads in Stone's cover story until each one petered out or ended in a blank wall. Not that it mattered. There was no one. Nick knew that for a fact. He looked out over the skyline of the city. Odd that Stone's life should have ended here, so close to where it had begun, across the water there in Birkenhead. Was it memories of those days that had made him so edgy on the journey up? Nick knew very little of the details—no one knew them, except possibly Leo—but he had been told enough to imagine a childhood spent between various council homes and unsuccessful attempts at fostering. There would be no blood relations to mourn the death of Peter Stone.

Six hours later he was back at Triple S headquarters. Control seemed unsurprised by his arrival and passed him through immediately to the private suite on the top floor. Pascoe was standing by the window, watching the opera-goers hurrying towards the Coliseum. He turned as Nick came in.

'Well?'

Nick met his eyes squarely. 'Stone's dead. Leonora shot him.'

If he had expected to see shock or distress on Pascoe's face he was disappointed. Only a momentary lowering of the heavy eyelids disturbed the mask. Pascoe gestured towards a chair.

'Tell me.'

Nick told him, sticking to the facts, his voice flat and level. He began to understand why Pascoe never showed any feelings. It was the only way it was possible to speak of these things at all. While he talked, Pascoe went to a side-table and poured them both a glass of brandy. When Nick had finished, he took a mouthful. It was good brandy, but it burnt his throat like raw spirit.

He looked at Pascoe, who was sitting now behind his desk. The room was growing dark and the reading lamp on the desk was switched on, illuminating the clean blotter, the paper-knife left ready for tomorrow's personal letters, but leaving his face in shadow.

'What now?"

'Now?' Pascoe spoke quietly. 'I suggest that you go home and get some sleep. Take some sleeping-pills, or half a bottle of Scotch, or whatever it takes. And then have four or five days leave. Come and see me next Monday and we'll decide whether you're ready to start work again.'

Nick stared at him, trying to penetrate the shadows and read those hooded eyes.

'But what are we going to do?'

'Clearly there is nothing we can do,' Pascoe returned. 'Stone is dead. We all know the risks which everyone in this organization runs—you as well as, perhaps better than, most. It's a shock, but it can hardly be a surprise. You can leave everything that needs to be done to me. I'll see that his belongings are channelled back here by some route, and get someone to clear his flat and see about terminating the lease etc. There wasn't anyone particular who should be informed, was there?'

Nick shook his head dumbly.

'I take it there is a will?'

Nick swallowed. 'Yes. With his bank.'

Pascoe was right. They had both known the chances of this happening to one or other of them and had discussed their arrangements.

'Oh', he added, 'and he wants to be cremated . . .' and then stopped abruptly as he realized what a ridiculous thing it was to say in

13

the circumstances.

Pascoe let it pass without comment. 'I'll keep in touch, of course, through various channels. If the body is found I'll make sure that we are informed.'

There was a silence. Nick waited for Pascoe to continue but he said nothing.

'And Leo?' Nick prompted.

'Leonora is in the hands of the law, and the law must take its course.'

Nick leaned forward. 'Do you mean that you're just going to leave her to it?'

Pascoe's voice did not waver. 'If Leonora has committed a crime, and confessed to that crime, then what do you expect me to do? She must pay the penalty.'

'Even if the penalty is twenty years in jail, or the rest of her life in a cell in Broadmoor?' Nick's voice was beginning to crack at last.

'If that is what the law decrees.'

'But surely you'll go and see her, make sure she has a good lawyer? Don't you want to know why she did it?'

'It would be most improper for me to become involved in any way. The integrity of the service must not be compromised.'

'So you're going to sit back here and let her go through all that on her own, without a single friend to help her?'

'Leo knew how sensitive the mission was. She knew that if anything went wrong Triple S could not become involved. She was in a better position to judge than you. She has preserved her cover. It would be worse than pointless for me to break it.'

Nick rose and his voice was thick and unsteady. 'You sent her there! You gave her this job! It was you who brought her into the service in the first place; you who persuaded her to live so many different lives that in the end she couldn't tell what was real and what was invention! And now you're going to let her rot—to "preserve the integrity of the service!" *What integrity?*'

Pascoe's hands were gripping the edge of the desk. In the lamplight Nick could see that the knuckles were white.

'At least let me go and see her,' he pleaded.

'Out of the question!' For the first time Pascoe raised his voice. 'You must see that any contact between you two is impossible. The police would immediately conclude that you were her accomplice.'

'Perhaps I was!' Nick was shouting now, his voice raw with unshed tears. 'Perhaps we both were! At least I'm prepared to share the rap with her. And you—you love her too,—for what it's worth!'

Pascoe's voice was quiet again, icy calm. 'I forbid you to contact Leonora in any way. That is an order.'

'An order?' Nick could feel his knees trembling. In spite of the years of hard training and harder experience the shock was

15

beginning to have its effect. He knew suddenly that if he did not get out within a minute or two he would break down completely. 'All right! If that's an order, than you can have my resignation!' He put his hand into the inside pocket of his jacket, feeling for the warrant card which usually lay there. Then he remembered that on this mission he had carried neither that nor his gun. 'You'll have my letter tomorrow.'

Pascoe's voice stopped him half-way to the door.

'Marriot! You will remember that, whether you are currently employed by the service or not, you are still bound by the undertakings that you gave when you joined. You have signed the Official Secrets Act'.

Nick drew a deep breath. He knew when he was beaten. He walked to the door and closed it quietly behind him.

CHAPTER TWO

'ACCUSED WOMEN ON HUNGER STRIKE'.

The newspaper placard hit Nick like a blow in the stomach. He hunched his shoulders and ducked his neck into the collar of his jacket as he bought a copy, as if the news-vendor might accuse him of being responsible. The warm

16

spell had come to an end and a cold rain spattered into his face as he turned into the Fulham Road and fumbled for his key.

Walking into the flat, he was aware briefly that if Stone could see it now his distaste would be real and well-founded. The living room was littered with empty glasses, mugs rimmed with the gluey remnants of coffee and plates on which the remains of two or three half-eaten meals were congealing. Through the open door to the bedroom the unmade bed spilled onto the carpet to join the dirty shirts and underwear which lay where they had fallen. The place stank of sweat and stale whisky.

Nick dropped into a chair, unwrapped the new bottle and reached for a glass. When he had swallowed a couple of gulps he opened the paper and found the report.

'Two women, each accused of separate murders, have gone on hunger strike while awaiting trial at the Risley Remand Centre on Merseyside. The women were named as Elizabeth Anne Walker, who is to be tried for the murder of sports goods rep Peter Stone in Liverpool ten days ago, and Margaret Mary Donelly, who is accused of the shooting of a security guard during the IRA attack on a Securicor van in the same city last month. Solicitors for the women said today that

17

the hunger strike was intended to draw attention to the fact that they refuse to accept the jurisdiction of the English courts and wish to be regarded as "prisoners of conscience". Donelly's political affiliations are, of course, clear since she freely admits to membership of the IRA, but those of Elizabeth Walker are rather more obscure. It appears that she is a member of an extreme feminist group calling itself "The Daughters of Sunrise" but little is known about the organisation except that it is dedicated to the overthrow of the present social structure by violent means. The women began their fast last night and say that they will continue it until their "special status" is recognised.'

Nick ran his hands over his face, becoming aware of a stubble of beard. When had he last shaved—two days ago, three? He could not remember, any more than he could remember when he had last eaten a proper meal. The last ten days had blurred into an indistinct recollection of getting drunk, sleeping, sobering up, starting to think and taking refuge in the bottle again, punctuated with spasmodic attempts to pull himself together. He had not sent in his letter of resignation, nor had he been into the office again. What Pascoe thought of the situation he neither knew nor cared.

He thrust his fingers into his hair and tried to force himself to concentrate on the report, convinced that here he might find a clue to the questions which had tormented him since Stone's death. He begun to reread it but in spite of himself his mind wandered off into memories of Leonora, which inevitably meant memories of Stone as well. 'Elizabeth Walker', eh? They hadn't broken her cover, then. He almost smiled at the thought of the field day the press would have if they knew who they were really dealing with. 'Ex-Actress on Murder Charge'; 'Mystery Star Accused of Shooting'. Although it was four years since she had made her only film she was still good for a photograph and a few lines in the gossip columns every time she attended a first night or dined out with a different man; and for those who remembered her previous stage career as a serious classical actress she was the occasion of many regretful sighs. Only half a dozen people in the world knew that Leonora Cavendish, stage name Leonora Carr, also known as Laura Cavendish, was an agent for Triple S; and, of those, fewer still knew the tragic story of how she had come to be one. [See *A Woman Called Omega.*]

It was just over a year ago that Nick and Stone had had their first encounter with her, and she had kept them wrong-footed for days by constantly changing her name and appearance until she finally decided to trust them. Since then she had appeared and disappeared, comet-like, in their lives; sometimes assigned by Pascoe to work with them on a case; sometimes ringing up one or other of them with a suggestion that they might accompany her to a concert, or have dinner at her Chelsea flat, or go with her on one of her less conventional escapades which might include anything from test-driving a new sports car to diving on a wreck; sometimes, infuriatingly, incommunicado, in the country cottage to which they were never invited. They each knew that they were both in love with her, and knew too that, while their love was not reciprocated, neither was it totally unrequited. Oddly enough, instead of arousing jealousy the situation had created an extra bond between them; only they had developed a kind of delicacy about asking each other what their plans were for the evening, or what they had done the night before.

Well, all that was over now. Nick reached for the whisky bottle, but then put it aside and instead got up and took a shower. He was shaving when the phone rang.

'Mr Marriot?' The cool, impersonal tone of the girl at Control was instantly recognizable. 'This is the Spartacus Health Club here. I have a message from Mr Pascoe. He would like to see you at the house in Hertfordshire.'

'Tell Mr Pascoe . . .' Nick began, then

changed his mind and put the phone down. Bloody typical of Pascoe, he thought, to leave him to stew all this time and then calmly assume that he would be ready to return to duty when summoned. Well, Pascoe could get knotted!

He looked at his face in the mirror. His eyelids were puffy, his eyes bloodshot and his skin, where it was emerging from under the stubble, looked like the underbelly of a particularly unhealthy frog. He finished shaving and went into the kitchen. There was nothing in the fridge, and a search through the cupboards produced only an esoteric collection of items, none of which seemed to relate to the others in any gastronomically acceptable way. In the end he settled for a tin of beans and the remains of a Christmas cake which had been presented to him by a nice old lady whose cottage they had used for a surveillance job last December. Somewhat to his surprise, by the time he had finished them he felt a good deal better. Taking advantage of the improvement he put the whisky bottle out of sight behind the cake tin and set about clearing up the flat. When it was done he stood by an open window and looked out. The rain had stopped and a golden gash in the clouds was angling slanting beams of sunlight across the wet roofs. The air touching his face was cool and moist and smelt of wet tarmac and the Thames. He closed the window, went into the bedroom and pulled out the overnight bag which was always ready packed at the bottom of the wardrobe. Fifteen minutes later he was on the A41, heading north.

The house in Hertfordshire was a Georgian building which had once been a farmhouse but had long ago lost all the land attached to it. It stood in a little copse of trees by a lane which wound its way across gently undulating country towards St Albans. Nick knew it well because it was often used as a safe house for 'guests' of Triple S who needed somewhere to stay out of the public eye. As he drove up to it the rose-red brick of the façade glowed in the warm light of the westering sun.

The door was opened to him by Waller, Pascoe's driver and bodyguard. He looked Nick over with an expression of impassive distaste and nodded towards a door.

'In there.'

Nick put down his bag and crossed towards the room which, in the house's palmier days, had been known as the library. He knocked and went in.

'You took your time!'

Nick stopped dead. The room faced west and the figure by the window was only an outline against the setting sun but the voice was unmistakable. He reached out and gripped the back of a chair. Once or twice during the last few days, going out for food or a fresh supply of whisky, he had experienced the phenomenon of an apparently familiar figure, half glimpsed among the crowd—something about the carriage of a head, or the colour of hair which produced a brief illusion of recognition; but this was altogether different and he was suddenly afraid that he had been hitting the whisky bottle harder even than he had realized.

His companion moved towards him, hiding concern under a show of amusement.

'Hey, come on,' said Stone, 'you're supposed to be pleased to see me!'

Nick felt his face go numb as the blood drained away from it and his hands shook so that the chair creaked at its joints. Stone muttered, 'Christ, Nick!' and moved away to a side-table. Nick heard the clink of bottle and glass and then smelt brandy as it was held under his nose. He looked down at the hand that held the glass—strong, short-fingered, the back of it lightly flecked with golden hairs. It reminded him of the time they had worked together defusing a bomb, working from directions given over the radio by an expert fifty miles away, their four hands moving in such close co-ordination that they might have belonged to one person. He could feel the faint warmth given off by Stone's body as he stood by his shoulder. This was no ghost. Slowly realization began to dawn.

'Pascoe!' Nick muttered between clenched teeth. 'Bloody Pascoe!'

He took the glass and raised it to his lips but the smell of it reminded him of his last conversation with his chief and he set it down again untouched. Slowly he turned and looked at Stone.

'If you ever do this to me again you bloody well will be dead, because I'll kill you myself! And then I'll go after Pascoe.'

The ice-blue eyes met his own with a glint of laughter.

'I've got a better idea. Do it the other way round, and I'll help you with Pascoe.'

Suddenly they were both laughing and Nick reached out and gripped his arm.

'When you've both quite finished disposing of my life . . .' Pascoe said smoothly from the doorway.

They turned to look at him.

'You're owed an explanation, Marriot,' Pascoe said. 'Let's sit down, shall we?'

It was the nearest he was likely to get to an apology, and Nick knew it. He looked from Pascoe to Stone.

'Do you know what's happening to Leo?'

'Of course I know!' Stone returned with some asperity.

'OK!' said Nick, his anger returning. 'So the whole thing was a fix. You know all about it. Presumably Leo knows all about it. Why was I kept in the dark?'

Pascoe moved over to the polished library table and sat down at the head of it. 'Sit down and let me explain.'

Torn between fury and curiosity Nick continued to stand gazing rebelliously from one to the other, until Stone put a warning hand behind his elbow and urged him towards the table.

'OK,' he said again, dropping into a chair. 'Leo didn't shoot you, so presumably you jumped. Then what?'

'I swam under the pier, hauled myself out the other side and Waller was waiting for me with a car and a change of clothes.'

'Bloody marvellous!' Nick gritted his teeth. 'So while I was sweating it out in the nick, you were comfortably tucked up in bed! So tell me, why was I the only one who didn't know what was going on?'

'We needed a witness,' Pascoe said. 'We couldn't produce a body for obvious reasons, and we thought it was unlikely that the police would charge Leonora simply because she was found with a gun in her hand. We had to have someone who would convince them that a murder had actually taken place.'

'I still don't see why I couldn't be told,' Nick protested.

'We just didn't think you were that good an actor,' Stone told him.

'All right, point taken,' Nick agreed unwillingly. 'But what about since then? Why couldn't I be told when I got back to London?'

'The police might have wanted to question

you again,' Pascoe pointed out reasonably. 'Though what they'd have got out of you, in the state you've been in the last ten days, is highly questionable, I should say.'

Nick glowered at him. 'You've had me watched!'

'I'd hardly let you drop out of sight for that long after what had happened,' Pascoe said mildly.

'So what's magic about today?' Nick demanded. 'Why am I suddenly permitted to rejoin the land of the living?'

'What is "magic" as you put it,' Pascoe said, 'is that we are now ready to proceed to the next phase of the operation.'

'I still don't know what the first phase was all about,' Nick muttered.

Pascoe leaned his elbows on the table and rested his chin on his folded hands. 'Let's take it from the top, as Leo would say. About three months ago we started to hear rumours from various sources that the IRA were planning something big for this summer. We couldn't find out any details, except that it was going to be in England and it was going to be quote the biggest shock since the assassination of Lord Mountbatten unquote. For some time we couldn't get a lead of any sort. Then the Merseyside police caught Margaret Donelly practically red-handed on that Securicor job. We'd heard that there was an IRA cell operating somewhere in the Liverpool area and we had picked up hints that their main job was to prepare for this major coup, whatever it is, so this was obviously a real opportunity. The trouble was that preliminary psychiatrists' reports suggested that Donelly was not the type who was going to break easily. However, we did discover that, as well as being a militant republican, she was also a militant feminist and it seemed to us that if we could get someone alongside her—another woman obviously—we might stand a better chance of learning something. We couldn't afford to wait until after the trial, so it had to be while she was on remand. It had to be quick, and it had to be murder, because prisoners accused of murder are kept apart from the others at Risley, in the hospital section. Hence the rather melodramatic scene at the Pier Head.'

'Incidentally,' Nick put in, 'how did the police get there so quickly?'

'Oh, the police received an anonymous tip-off that a shipment of drugs were coming ashore in that area that night. They didn't find any, of course, but it made sure that they were out in strength.'

'I still can't see,' Stone put in, as if returning to a previously argued point, 'why Donelly should trust anyone just because she happened to be accused of murder too.'

'Well, there were various factors in our favour,' Pascoe said. 'Obviously, it had to be the right sort of murder—i.e. a politically motivated one. Hence the "Daughters of the Sunrise".'

'You mean they were a complete invention?' Nick queried.

'Oh, a total figment of the imagination,' Pascoe agreed. 'Leo thought of the name, actually.'

'I might have guessed,' Stone muttered and Nick caught his eye and felt the first stirrings of a hitherto unrecognized joy.

'What other factors?' he asked Pascoe.

'Well, obviously anyone in that position feels isolated, vulnerable—a woman more so than a man. Leo will have played upon their mutual dislike of the present government, indeed of all authority and on their hatred of the police and their contempt for men in general. That is her strongest card, given what we know about Donelly.'

Stone looked at Pascoe, 'You mean Donelly is a Lesbian.'

'According to our sources.'

Once again Stone and Nick exchanged glances. Then Stone rose abruptly and moved away to the window.

'And you expect Leo to go along with that?'

'Leonora is a very clever woman. She can take care of herself.'

'Yes?' Nick put in. 'What about this hunger strike?'

For the first time Pascoe looked slightly uneasy. 'That was not part of the original plan,

28

and I haven't yet been able to discover how it started. However, you can be assured that Leo will be instructed to call it off at once.'

'You're in touch with her then?' Nick asked.

'Naturally. Her solicitor is one of our own men. He'll see her tomorrow and put a stop to it.'

Stone came back to the table. 'You mean he'll try. You know as well as we do that Leo has no equal when it comes to sheer bloody-mindedness. She's just as likely to carry on to prove that she can stick it as long as the other woman!'

'In that case,' Pascoe said imperturbably, 'Donelly will have to be persuaded to come off it too. I may have to arrange for a few cosmetic concessions to enable them to save face and to retain Leo's credibility. But Leo knows that we need her on top form for the next phase. She'll see sense.'

'And the next phase is . . . ?' Nick prodded.

'I'm sure you will both be delighted to hear that the next step is to get Leo out of prison again.'

Stone grinned broadly. 'That's the best thing I've heard all evening—even considering all the trouble I went to to get her in.'

'*You* went to!' Nick exclaimed.

'That water was very cold—and extremely dirty,' Stone returned, looking injured.

'Does this mean that Leo's got the information we want already?' Nick asked.

Pascoe shook his head. 'Far from it, I'm afraid. We never imagined it was going to be that easy. You will be freeing not only Leo but Donelly as well.'

For a long moment Stone and Nick regarded Pascoe in silence. At length Stone said,

'You mean spring them?'

'If that's the term you want to use.'

'Great!' said Nick. 'Then we can all go to jail.'

'You do know,' Stone pointed out, 'that contriving the escape of a prisoner charged with murder is a very serious offence?'

'Of course I know!' said Pascoe tetchily. 'Believe me, it is not something I would advocate except in very exceptional circumstances. And it has been cleared at the very highest level.'

'Ah,' Stone looked relieved, 'then we can rely on the tacit co-operation of the local police.'

'I'm afraid not. I said the operation had been cleared at the very highest level. That does not mean that it has been discussed with the copper on the beat—or with his Chief Constable, for that matter! This is strictly a Triple S affair. You can have any resources in terms of man-power or materials you want from the Department, but apart from that the whole thing is down to you. Just don't let it go wrong!'

'I don't get it,' Nick said. 'What, exactly, is the idea?'

'Hopefully, that Donelly and Leo will go on the run together and that Donelly will eventually take Leo back to a safe house somewhere where they can link up with the rest of the group.'

'But who is Donelly supposed to think is behind the rescue?' Stone asked. 'Obviously, she'll know it isn't her own lot.'

'Quite,' Pascoe nodded, 'but that is why we have built up this imaginary revolutionary group of Leo's so carefully. Although it is primarily a women's organization, it does have male members too and it has been secretly preparing for armed struggle. In other words, it has the arms and the command structure to stage a rescue attempt. This is what Leo will have been telling Donelly. In fact, she will have told her that the solicitor is working for them and will warn her when the attempt is to take place—as in fact he will.'

'So, as far as Donelly is concerned, we are members of the "Daughters of the Sunrise",' Nick said.

'Well,' Pascoe permitted himself a small smile, 'associate members, perhaps.'

'In that case,' Stone objected, 'surely we would have arranged a safe house of some kind, or transport out of the country.'

'Of course, you will have done,' Pascoe agreed, 'and you will endeavour to persuade

Leo—or Elizabeth, as we must call her—to fall in with your plans. She, however, will insist that she is going to stick with Donelly. Apart from any—emotional—bond which they may have formed she will have allowed Donelly to convince her of the rightness of her cause and she will evince an ardent desire to work for the IRA. You will probably have quite an argument with her, but ultimately she will go with Donelly.'

'Provided Donelly will have her,' Stone said.

'You need not worry about that. Leo has already indicated that she is pretty sure on that point—otherwise I should not have initiated phase two.'

'But surely Donelly will head straight back for Ireland,' Nick said.

'We shall make very sure that there is heavy surveillance on all ports and crossings,' Pascoe told him. 'And Leo will be quick to point out that that is the quickest way to get picked up again. Their best bet will be to lie low—and we want to know where, and with whom. From the moment that the break takes place they will be under surveillance, both on the ground and from the air. Stone, you had better handle that end of it. I want you airborne, controlling the surveillance teams.'

'We've got to get them out first,' Nick pointed out.

'They are taken every Thursday from Risley to Liverpool to appear in court. The road in places is very quiet. I should say that that would be your best bet. The details are up to you.' Pascoe looked at his watch. 'I have to get back to London. Mrs Fitch will serve you dinner in half an hour. You will find all that you are likely to need in the way of maps in the drawers of that bureau and, of course, for any other information you have access to the central computer at Control via the terminal in the next room. Work out your plan, and what personnel you require, and let me know as soon as you can.'

They accompanied Pascoe to the door and watched him drive away. As they turned back into the hall, Stone looked at Nick.

'Where the hell have you been?' he asked. 'I'm the one who's supposed to be dead, but you look like the one who's been buried for ten days!'

*   *   *

It was around midnight that Stone exclaimed, 'What we want is more security, not less!'

'Come again?' Nick said sleepily.

They had talked through dinner and on over pot after pot of coffee. Nick was dog tired but he knew that he would not sleep until they had at least the germ of an idea about how to release Leo and her fellow prisoner.

'Listen,' Stone said. 'We've agreed that the attempt has got to be made during the drive from Risley to court, or back again. The prisoners travel in a special van, each one locked into a separate cell inside. There's a driver and another officer in the front, who are in radio contact with the prison. If the van is stopped for any reason all they have to do is lock the doors and radio for help, unless . . .'

'Unless?' Nick prompted.

Stone grinned at him. 'Can you still fit into that copper's uniform of yours?'

'About as well as you fit into your RAF uniform, I should think,' Nick returned. 'What am I supposed to do, climb into a panda car and flag them down for speeding?'

'Jam butty,' Stone said.

'At this time of night?'

'No, idiot. That's what they call panda cars in Liverpool—jam butty cars.'

Nick put his head in his hands. 'I'm lost,' he moaned.

Stone tapped him on the knuckles with his pen.

'Pay attention, you're dozing off! We need to find a way of stopping the van that won't arouse their suspicions. Suppose they were told to expect a police escort? They wouldn't know that you aren't a Liverpool copper.'

'As long as I don't open my mouth,' Nick muttered.

Stone sat back, chewing the end of his biro. 'It's not the whole answer, though. We not only need to stop them, we need to get them out of the van. How do we do that?'

There was no response. He prodded the mop of tousled curls with the end of the pen but there was no reaction. Nick was dead to the world.

CHAPTER THREE

Three days later, in a pub in Knowsley on the outskirts of Liverpool, a frail, bird-boned little man accepted a pint of Guinness from a larger man in a dark raincoat.

'Well, Michael?' the large man asked. 'What's it all about?'

The little man took a long pull at his stout and wiped the froth from his mouth with the back of his hand.

'It's not much, you know,' he murmured, leaning towards his companion and projecting a halitosis as lethal as a ray gun in his direction. 'It's only a rumour.'

'A rumour about what?' The big man controlled the urge to turn his head away.

'This girl you've got in Risley—the Irish girl . . .'

The big man's eyes narrowed and he forgot the halitosis.

'What about her?'

'The word's out that they're after getting her away.'

'Springing her—from Risley?'

'I can't give you any details. Like I said, it's just a rumour.'

The policeman put his hand into his pocket and then laid it casually on the table between them. The edges of several notes were just visible beneath his fingers.

'You have to bring her into the city once a week, don't you?' The little man watched the hand like a cat waiting to pounce on a bird. 'I don't know—I can't be sure—but I should look out for trouble on the drive.'

The hand on the table was lifted and another, like a quick paw, snatched up the notes. The little man drained his glass, apparently without pausing to swallow, and was gone, scuttling away between the tables. The policeman watched him go and then settled back into his seat to finish his own drink and scan the copy of the *Echo* which was tucked into his raincoat pocket. The article which immediately attracted his attention was about half-way down the front page.

RISLEY WOMEN END HUNGER STRIKE.
The two women accused of murder who are being held at the Risley remand centre gave up their five day old hunger strike today after being visited by a Catholic priest . . .'

The big man read the report through carefully, finished his beer and made his way out into the grey city dusk.

The rumour was duly reported and the report passed from desk to desk until eventually a memo returned to the chief inspector to the effect that the Government was anxious not to attract too much public attention to the case of Margaret Donelly, who was obviously intent on manipulating the media, probably for the benefit of IRA sympathizers in the United States. Any extra precautions should therefore be as low key as possible. It was decided that on its next journey the prison van should have the benefit of an escorting police car, to clear the way and ensure that it had no need to stop for any reason.

The man given the job of driving this escort vehicle was Bill Lithgow, a sergeant with nearly twenty years' service behind him. His companion was Constable Stephen Carney, a well-built, hard-looking young man who prided himself on being 'useful' in a fight.

'What d'you reckon, Sarge?' he asked as they set off. 'What do we do if the micks try to jump us?'

'Listen,' the older man returned, 'forget the heroics. All we have to do is drive to Risley, pick up the van and then head back here without stopping for anybody.'

'Suppose they blow us up?' Carney

demanded. 'How do we know they haven't put a bomb in a culvert or something?'

'Wouldn't do them any good. They don't want to risk damaging the van, do they? They might end up killing their own girl. If anything happens to us all the two officers in the van have got to do is sit tight, keep the doors locked and radio for help.'

'Well, what do you think they are going to do, then?' Carney seemed quite disappointed by his companion's sanguine attitude.

'Nothing,' retorted Lithgow. 'That's my bet.' He glanced sideways at the constable's eager profile. 'Anyway, if anything does happen it'll be on the way back, after we've collected the van; so relax, can't you. You're making me feel uncomfortable.'

They were within about five miles of their destination when they saw a man come out of a side turning and start running along the road towards them. He paused for an instant on the kerb as if intending to cross the road to a phone-box on the other side, then saw them and stepped out, waving his arms for them to stop. Lithgow was forced to break sharply to avoid hitting him.

'Now what?' he muttered, as the car came to a standstill.

The man darted round to the front passenger window and leaned in. He was about 30, dressed in jeans and a donkey jacket, his face red with exertion.

'Thank Christ you came along, mate!' he panted. 'I was heading for that phone-box to call you.'

'What is it?' Lithgow asked long-sufferingly. 'Wife gone into labour unexpectedly, has she?'

The man looked slightly put out. 'No, it's nothing like that. There's only a bloke down there with a shot-gun, threatening to blow himself and his two kids to kingdom come, isn't there.'

Lithgow sat forward sharply. 'Down there? Where?'

'In a house down the lane there—Willow Cottage. He lives there.'

'Who is he? Do you know him?'

'Yeah. His name's Askew—Ron Askew. Look, hadn't we better get down there? He sent me to call the police but he said if I wasn't back in ten minutes he wouldn't answer for the consequences.'

Lithgow leaned over and unlocked the rear door. 'Get in.'

The man climbed in but Lithgow did not immediately start the engine.

'You say he's threatening to shoot the kids, and himself? Why?'

' 'Cos his wife's left him. He works nights, see. Apparently, he came home this morning and found the kids tucked up in bed asleep and a note from his wife saying she'd gone off with another bloke and he'd never see her again.'

'How do you know all this?' asked Carney, who had been itching to get a word in.

'I live up the road a bit, see,' the man answered. 'I was walking down this morning to get the bus to work and just as I was passing his place he yells out to me from the bedroom window. To start with I thought perhaps one of them was ill or something, but when I got inside the garden gate he points this shot-gun at me and tells me not to come no nearer. Then he told me about Gillian—that's his wife—and said to come and phone for you boys.'

'Why?' asked Lithgow. 'What does he want us for?'

'What he said was—call the police, call the *Echo*, call Radio City and Radio Merseyside, and Granada TV. I want them all here. Tell them unless my wife's back here by ten o'clock tonight I'm going to blast the kids' heads off and then my own. I don't know where she's gone, he says, but I want to make sure she sees the reports. That'll get her back here. Look, can't we get moving? He's in a right state, I can tell you. If he thinks I've pushed off and left him to it God knows what he'll do.'

'D'you know him—personally, I mean,' asked Lithgow. 'Is he the sort of man who might do a thing like that, or is it all bluff?'

The man pursed his lips. 'Hard to say, isn't it. I mean, I never thought of him as a nutter, like. But he can be violent, I know that. And he's always been terrible jealous of Gillian. The wife and me used to go out with them sometimes, but we give it up 'cos he used to make these awful scenes if another man so much as looked at her. No telling what he might do now.'

Lithgow sighed. 'All right. We'd better go and have a look. Down to the left, is it?' He started the engine. 'Call in, Steve. Tell 'em what's going on and ask them to send someone out to take over.'

Carney pressed the transmit button on the microphone.

'Tango Able Foxtrot to Control. Am investigating a report of a man with a shot-gun holding children hostage in Willow Cottage, Moss Lane. Request another car to take over from us. Out.'

*   *   *

In a large barn, some two hundred yards further along the main road, Nick Marriot heard the message over the radio in a white Rover painted with the broad red stripe and the crest of the Merseyside police.

'Did you get that, Vince?' he asked of the man beside him.

'No problem!' Vince replied. 'Tango Able Foxtrot to Control—you have just been had!' The voice was an exact reproduction of the flat, nasal scouse which was Carney's normal speech.

Nick grinned and wondered whether Pascoe made a habit of recruiting his agents from the world of showbusiness. He shifted his position, aware that the waistband of his uniform suit was a little tighter than when he had last had it on some four years back.

'Tango Able Foxtrot,' came Carney's voice over the radio. 'Have reached Willow Cottage. No sign of trouble from here. Off watch to investigate. Out.'

'Give them five minutes,' said Nick.

* * *

The police car was stopped a short distance from the cottage, partly concealed by a hedge. Lithgow peered up at the top windows.

'Which room did you say?'

'The bedroom. Top right-hand window.'

'No sign of movement there at the moment.'

'He's probably keeping his head down,' said Carney.

'You stay here, Mr . . . What is your name, sir?' Lithgow inquired.

'Fenton—Harry Fenton.'

'Right, Mr Fenton. You stay here and we'll go and have a word with him.'

'OK,' the man replied. 'But go careful. I've told you, he's in a right state.'

The two policemen approached the gate cautiously. There was still no sign of

42

movement in the upper window.

Lithgow called, 'Mr Askew?—Mr Askew, we're police officers. You wanted to talk to us.'

There was no reply. Lithgow led the way up the path and then, after a brief conference, Carney moved away to the back of the house.

Lithgow tried again. 'Mr Askew. We want to help you. Are you there?'

He glanced round towards the car. Fenton had got out and was standing by the driver's door, watching them. Carney reappeared from behind the house. Turning to speak to him Lithgow did not see Fenton bend quickly and reach a gloved hand under the dashboard.

'No sign of life round there, Sarge,' Carney reported.

Lithgow stepped back and scanned the upstairs windows again. Then he knocked on the door.

'Mr Askew! I must ask you to open this door!'

'Oh Christ! I hope he hasn't done anything!' Fenton was standing by the gate now.

'You keep back, Mr Fenton,' Lithgow called. 'Come on, Constable, let's have this door open.'

The cottage door was not very strong and a few hefty kicks from Carney splintered the lock. There was no sound from inside the house and after a cursory glance into the two downstairs rooms the two men began to edge up the stairs. They were on the upper landing when they heard the car start up. From the window they saw it reverse into a gateway and turn round. By the time they reached the garden gate only the ripples in the puddles showed where it had passed.

*   *   *

The barn doors slid open and the white and red car nosed out and headed towards Risley.

'Tango Able Foxtrot,' said Carney's voice, issuing from Vince's mouth. 'False alarm. Cancel the reinforcements. I'll explain in my report. On our way. Out.'

Switching to a different wavelength Nick reported, 'Delta One, this is Delta Two. All systems are go so far. We are on our way. Over.'

In a Triple S radio van parked on the edge of Speke Airport Stone replied, 'Delta Two, this is Delta One. Good luck. Out.'

'Harry Fenton', whose real name was Max Urquahart, parked the stolen police car neatly in a lay-by three or four miles from Willow Cottage and retuned the radio.

'Delta One, this is Theta One. Pinky and Perky have lost their wheels and they've got a long walk ahead of them. Over.'

'Theta One,' Stone replied, 'Delta One here. Well done. What about the phone-box?'

'Delta One—don't worry, I fixed it. They'll have to get a lift to the next one. Am proceeding to my next station. Out.'

He carefully returned the radio to its normal frequency, got out of the car and into a red Cavalier which was parked just ahead of it, and drove away in the direction of the M6.

*　　*　　*

At the remand centre the prison van was waiting to start its journey. The driver looked at his watch.

'They're late,' he commented morosely.

'Not very,' said his companion.

'Not yet. But you know what it'll be. If we get held up anywhere and the prisoners aren't there to be put up when they're wanted, we're the ones who are going to get it in the neck—not them.'

'But that's the whole point, isn't it?' the other man said. 'We won't get held up with them in front of us—not by anything.'

'Huh!' was the only comment.

'Here they are, anyway,' continued the second man, as the white and red Rover swung in through the gates.

The police car executed a neat turn and pulled past the van, waving them to follow.

'Not hanging about, are they?' said the second man.

'I should bloody well think not!' returned the driver as he let in the clutch and followed the car out of the gates.

There was not very much traffic on the road and the police car lead them at a good speed towards the city. They did not particularly notice a Gas Board van parked beside the road and were not aware that immediately after they had passed two men got out and set up a Road Closed notice and another warning of a possible gas leak. Nor did they have any means of knowing that at a junction just ahead an articulated lorry had jack-knifed, effectively sealing off that section of road from the other direction.

As they passed the barn from which the Rover had started its journey Nick glanced at Vince in the passenger seat beside him.

'Brace yourself!'

He reached out and pushed a button on the dashboard in front of him. There was a muffled explosion and the car skidded wildly to the left, almost wrenching the steering-wheel out of Nick's grasp. It mounted the pavement, rocked as if about to turn over and finally collided with a tree and came to rest. Both men were thrown violently forward and lay without moving, while a wisp of steam began to curl up from under the bonnet.

Behind them the van had also braked to a sudden halt, to the accompaniment of expletives and warning shouts from the two prison officers,

'Watch out!' shouted the driver.

'Where are they?' demanded the other.

46

'Was it a shot?'

They sat tensely, staring around them. There was no sign of movement. The road and the fields around were empty. Ahead, the two men in the car lay slumped against the dashboard.

'We ought to give them a hand,' said the second officer.

'Sit tight!' ordered the driver. 'We don't know who's out there.'

His companion leaned forward. 'Hang about, one of them's moving.'

They watched as the driver of the car slowly dragged himself out of the wreckage, clutching his right arm to him, apparently useless. He limped round the vehicle and tried the opposite door, but it failed to open. Then he turned and came over to the van. He was swaying as if about to faint and a trickle of blood ran from the corner of his mouth. The second guard opened his window.

'Give me a hand, can't you?' the policeman said. 'I can't get the door open and the car could go up any minute.'

'Who's out there?' demanded the driver. 'Who shot at you?'

'Nobody shot at us,' the man in sergeant's uniform said through clenched teeth. 'We had a blow-out.'

The second guard jumped down from the van. 'You hop in, mate,' he said. 'I'll get your pal out.'

The sergeant hauled himself into the passenger seat, while the guard ran over to the car and jerked at the door. The man inside was unconscious, lying against the door. The prison officer yanked again and the door opened, spilling the limp body out at his feet. It was when he stooped to raise it that he found his neck caught in a fierce grip.

'All right, mate, all right!' he gasped.

For answer, a foot was braced in his stomach and he found himself turning a near somersault to end up flat on his back with the man he had rescued kneeling on his chest. At the same instant the sergeant in the van suddenly recovered the use of his right arm and thrust an automatic against the side of the driver's neck.

'Out!' he said tersely.

Within seconds the two guards found themselves handcuffed and hustled into the barn. Then, while Vince kept watch over them, Nick backed the van inside and unlocked it with the keys he had taken from the driver.

'Elizabeth?' he called.

'Here!' the voice answered at once, clear, vibrant—almost painfully familiar.

He unlocked the door of the cell. She was on her feet already. The five-day fast had pared away the flesh of her face and left the skin as translucent as the shell of a robin's egg, but the eyes were alight with triumph and for a second the old Leo stood looking at him. Then he saw her face change and harden, as if she had put on a mask. She pushed past him and went to the door of another cell.

'Open this one—quick!'

He unlocked it and once again she shouldered him aside to get to the other prisoner. Margaret Donelly was small, stockily built, with dark hair cut in a heavy fringe which almost hid her eyes—eyes which looked out at the world with a habitual expression of burning resentment; except, as Nick discovered, when they were focused on Leo.

'It's all right, Meg,' Leo was saying. 'They're my people. I told you they were coming.'

Nick moved to the door of the van. 'Quick, come on!'

Parked next to the van was a white Transit with the name of a firm of builders on it. The two girls moved to the door after him and he made to offer his hand to help Leo down. She brusquely ignored it, as did Donelly. He opened the back of the Transit.

'Get in. There's a change of clothes for both of you, and a couple of wigs. Yours are in the blue bag L—Liz.' He caught himself just in time. He had almost called her Leo. 'In case we're stopped, you're a couple of hitch-hikers heading for the Lake District and we picked you up outside the University at nine o'clock.'

Leo nodded briefly and the two women climbed into the Transit. Nick shut the door on them, struggled out of his uniform and into

49

a pair of dungarees and went round to the driver's seat. Vince, already changed, had pushed the prison officers into the back of their own van and locked it. He opened the door of the barn and closed it behind the Transit as Nick drove it out.

Nick was speaking over the radio. 'Delta One, this is Delta Two. The pigeons are free—heading east. Out.'

In the communications van parked by the airport Stone turned to Mitch, the Triple S Field Communications Officer.

'Time I was airborne. Call Kappa One and Kappa Two, will you, and tell them to pack up and move on. I'll keep in touch.'

A minute later the driver of the articulated lorry suddenly discovered a way of unscrambling his vehicle; and the Gas Board men decided that the gas leak was a false alarm and reopened the road, just in time to allow the passage of a white builders' van.

Vince grinned at Nick and rubbed his neck ruefully. 'You sure don't do things by halves, do you. You know, for a bit there I thought those two sods were going to leave us there to fry.'

Nick nodded. 'They were quite right, of course.'

'I'm glad you convinced them otherwise,' Vince commented. 'That must have been a very effective bit of acting you put on.'

Nick grinned and jerked his head towards

the back of the van. 'I've had a pretty good coach!'

The panel between the driving seat and the goods compartment slid open.

'Where are we going?' Leo demanded, in the harsh, clipped voice which was so unlike her natural one that it made Nick wince.

'Lake District,' he returned. 'We've found a place there—farmhouse, very isolated. You'll be able to lie low until the heat's off.'

'No,' she said sharply. 'I'm sticking with Margaret.'

'She can come too.'

'We're not going to skulk in some farmhouse doing nothing. Meg wants to get back to her own people, and I'm going with her.'

'Don't be daft! All her people were picked up after that Securicor job. There can't be a safe house left in Liverpool.'

'Not Liverpool, you fool! You don't think that's the only Irish community in Britain, do you?'

'Where then?'

'Never mind. Just drop us at the first service station on the M6. We'll look after ourselves from there.'

'But Liz . . .' he protested.

'Don't whine!' she snapped. 'And don't call me Liz!'

The panel closed with a bang. Vince glanced sideways at Nick, pursed his lips and shook his knuckles as if they had been rapped. Nick grinned.

'You should see her when she's really mad,' he said softly.

The Cessna took off from Speke and climbed rapidly, circling eastwards. Stone picked out the line of the East Lancs Road and followed it. There was plenty of traffic now, and more than one white van; but the special scanner in the aircraft soon picked out the broad cross painted in ultra-violet paint on the roof of Nick's vehicle. Stone overflew it, circled and came back, watching as it turned south onto the M6. He turned his radio to transmit.

'Theta One, pigeons are heading in your direction. Stay put. Theta Two, Kappa One, move south. Acknowledge.'

One by one the acknowledgments came back. Below the circling aircraft the Gas Board van also headed towards the motorway while to the north a black Sierra pulled out of a lay-by and made for Junction 24.

Nick swung the van into the car-park of the Knutsford service area and stopped. The girls scrambled out of the back. Both had changed into jeans and anoraks and carried rucksacks; and both had put on wigs which radically changed their appearance. Leo now had long auburn hair and Donelly's was light brown and curly, but whereas it had the effect of making her look more than ever like a mutinous

Shetland pony Leo appeared more fragile and ethereal than before.

Nick said, 'Change your mind, come with us!'—and meant it.

For a second her eyes met his and he knew how much she would have liked to agree. Then she said,

'I've told you. I've got more important things to do. I'll be in touch—when I'm ready.'

The girls shouldered their packs and began to move away towards the slip-road leading back onto the motorway. For a second Leo paused and looked back.

'That was an efficient operation—well done.'

Nick watched them out of sight and then climbed back into the van and reached for his microphone.

'Delta One, this is Delta Two. Our friends are thumbing a lift at the Knutsford Services—southbound. Better make it snappy. I don't think they'll have to wait long.'

Circling above him Stone acknowledged the call and tuned a knob on a small receiver. A steady bleep told him that the homing device sewn into Leo's clothes was working at full power.

'Theta One,' he called. 'This is Delta One. The carrier pigeons are waiting to be picked up. On your way.'

On the far side of the car-park from the builders' van the red Cavalier pulled out and set off down the slip-road, to stop a few seconds later just beyond a pair of hitch-hikers.

'Where to, girls?' inquired Max Urquahart.

Nick and Vince did not have to wait very long before the communications van pulled into a parking slot a few yards away. They joined Mitch in the back of it.

'What happened to you?' he asked, and Nick realized that he still had a trickle of dried stage blood running down his chin.

Mitch, always well provided for operations of this nature, produced sandwiches and a thermos of coffee and while they ate they listened to Stone's occasional, laconic reports as the Cavalier headed steadily southwards, and the bleeping of the homing device. Then they heard Stone say,

'Stand by, Kappa Two. Theta One leaving at Junction 9.'

A minute after Max Urquahart had dropped his passengers on the Dudley road a Gas Board van slowed down just long enough for one of its occupants, a tall, loose-limbed black man in a boiler suit, to jump out. He saw the two girls ahead of him and strolled after them and when they stopped at a bus stop he joined the queue. As they waited he noticed a black Sierra glide past in the traffic, but he did not make any gesture of recognition. Later, when they had boarded the bus, he saw it pull out of a side turning and squeeze into the line of cars about three behind.

In the communications van Mitch tuned into the 11 a.m. news bulletin on Radio 4 and they heard the first report of the escape. 'Police road-blocks have been set up all round the area,' said the news-reader.

'Control, this is Theta Two,' said a voice from the set still tuned to the Triple S frequency. 'The pigeons have reached Tipton. I think they're nearly home.'

Nick got out of the van and found a phone-box. He called the Merseyside police and told them where to find the two prison officers, ringing off quickly before they could trace the call.

'Viv' Vivian, alias Kappa Two, paused to gaze into the window of a newsagent's shop and saw in its reflection a dapper-looking young man carrying a brief-case jump out of the black Sierra and set off briskly down the road. A hundred yards further on the two girls turned into a side-road. Viv smiled to himself and caught a bus back to his rendezvous with the Gas Board van.

The dapper young man, who answered to the code name of Theta Two, stopped a couple of housewives and involved them in answering a market survey questionnaire which he produced from his brief-case. While they talked he watched the two girls. They stopped at the door of a small, terraced house and rang the bell. After a moment the door was opened by a thin, dark man. A few words were spoken and then all three disappeared quickly inside. Theta Two thanked the housewives and put the questionnaire back in his case, activating as he did so a small radio transmitter.

'Delta One, this is Theta Two,' came the call. 'I am in Daltry Road, Tipton. The pigeons have gone to roost.'

'Understood, Theta Two,' Stone replied. 'Stand by. Kappa One will join you shortly.'

Twenty minutes later the Gas Board van turned into the street and set up a little tent over a section of road some fifty yards away from the house on the far side. Inside, Barney Lightfoot, Kappa One, checked that the homing device still registered that its wearer was stationary and then he and Viv Vivian settled down to wait for further instructions. The young man in the Sierra gave up questioning passers-by about their breakfast habits and went off to lunch.

Nick picked Stone up at Birmingham airport. They were due to meet Pascoe for lunch at the Excelsior.

'How was Leo?' Stone asked.

Nick made a rueful face. 'Looking like gossamer and behaving like a barbed-wire entanglement,' he said.

Stone grinned. 'That figures,' he agreed.

CHAPTER FOUR

Leo heard the lock on the door of the shabby front bedroom turn softly behind her and permitted herself a small, grim smile. Whatever Margaret Donelly said in her favour, it was hardly to be expected that she would be accepted straight away—if at all. She sat down on the edge of one of the two narrow beds and pulled off the auburn wig, running her fingers through her cropped hair. She was more tired than she could ever remember. She thought of Nick, standing in the sunlight in the service area car-park, his mobile, humorous face surrounded by the halo of reddish-brown curls which always made him look, to her, like a Renaissance prince, saying, 'Come with us.' If only she could have done! If only that had been the end, instead of just the beginning . . .

She got up and took off her coat and then began a systematic search for the electronic bugs which she knew would be somewhere among the clothes she had been given. It was as well to know, so that she could be sure that she was always carrying at least one—and to see that no one else had a chance to find them. She located them at length; one sewn into the base of the auburn wig, and another masquerading as a stud on the pocket of her jeans. She dressed again and moved cautiously to the window. The sight of the Gas Board van was reassuring. She was just wondering who was manning it when Barney Lightfoot stepped out into the sunlight and lit a cigarette. His gaze casually swept the houses opposite and lingered for a moment on her window. Neither of them made a sign, but it was sufficient for them both to know that they had made contact. Leo suppressed a small feeling of disappointment. She knew that Nick must not be seen in the area, after this morning, but she had hoped that it might be Stone out there.

Downstairs in the back kitchen Margaret Donelly, white-faced but rebellious, was confronting Kevin Reilly, the tall man who had let them in.

'What else was I to do? Her people got me out, didn't they? It was more than any of you would have done!'

'Let her stay with her people! What call did you have to bring her here?'

'I told you! We made a vow in the prison hospital, when we were both half dead with hunger; we vowed that if we ever got free we'd stick together.'

'Half dead with hunger!' he scoffed. 'Five days you were on hunger strike—five days! There are men who've fasted for thirty and more, and well you know it!'

'So when did you go for five days without food?' she shouted back. 'And she would have gone on, if I hadn't begged her to give up. It was only when I told her that Father Martin had threatened me with hell-fire if I went on that she agreed. I told her that I wouldn't stop unless she did, and she said that nothing on this earth would make her give those pigs the satisfaction of seeing her give up, but she wouldn't endanger my immortal soul. I tell you, Kevin, that woman is made of the stuff of holy martyrs. She's like a white-hot flame, and worth ten of any man I ever met!'

'But why did you have to bring her here?' he hissed. 'Can't you see you put us all at risk?'

'And where else should I have gone?' she demanded. 'Wasn't it you who first brought me over from Ireland?'

'And I'm more than glad to see you. But not her! What are we to do with her? We can't hide her here indefinitely.'

'She wants to help—to help us, to help the cause. When we've finished what we came here for, she can come back to Ireland with us.'

There was a silence in which he studied her face for a long moment. At length he sighed.

'Well, we'll see what the others have to say when they come in. Meanwhile, you'll both stay hidden. Keep away from windows, and pray the police haven't already picked up your trail! We'll have to think of a story about who you are and where you come from. Now fetch her down and I'll find you both something to eat.'

The two women spent the afternoon lying on the narrow beds in the front room, dozing fitfully. Leo listened to the intermittent chatter of the pneumatic drill outside and wondered how big a hole Barney and Viv were going to dig. Perhaps it was just their way of letting her know they were still there.

Around half-past five the door bell rang and Leo heard the voices of two more men in the hall. These, she knew from Margaret, must be Patrick and Liam Connor who shared the house with Reilly and worked at a local factory. Reilly himself was, officially, unemployed. After a while Reilly called Margaret down and ten minutes later she returned to fetch Leo.

Entering the kitchen Leo experienced a sensation which was far from unfamiliar to her—the electric sense that the men in the room were stunned into silent appreciation, Reilly, she knew, had disliked and distrusted her on sight. She was not quite sure why, but the feeling was mutual. The faces of the two Connor brothers told a different story. She glanced from one to the other and read something in the eyes of the elder one, Patrick, that sent a tingle down her spine. Well, she reflected, it could be useful, but with her present cover it would have to be handled carefully.

'Sit down,' Reilly said curtly. 'We've a few

questions to ask you.'

Leo sat, steeling herself for the cross-examination.

'Elizabeth Walker—is that your real name?'

'Yes. Why shouldn't it be?'

'Where were you born?'

'In Zimbabwe. My father owned a farm out there. We sold up and came back here just before independence.'

(It was a useful cover story and Triple S agents often used a version of it. It made it so much more difficult for anyone to check the facts beyond a few years back.)

'Can you prove any of that?'

She shrugged. 'Obviously not. The police have all my documents. Unless you feel like asking them . . .'

'This man Stone, did you really shoot him?'

'Yes. I've never denied it.'

'Why?'

'He was one of them—a pig, in every sense of the word. He'd been trying to infiltrate the organization. The fool was so sure no woman could resist him! There was only one reason he could think of why I should want to meet him at that time of night.' She laughed briefly. 'It was worth it all just to see the look on his face when I pulled the gun!'

'This organization of yours—I've never heard of it. Tell me about it.'

'Of course you've never heard of it. It's run by women, not men. We don't go round blabbing about what we're going to do. We get on and do it.'

'Do what, for example?'

'For example—lift one of your people out from under the noses of the pigs. I didn't see you trying it.'

'According to what I've heard it was two men who conducted that operation.' Reilly sounded distinctly nettled.

Leo was prepared for this one.

'Men are useful—even necessary—for certain jobs. No one would have believed in two policewomen turning up as escorts. We have several men who understand our ideas and are prepared to work for us. But the organization and planning are all done by women.'

'And where are your headquarters?'

Leo gave him a steady look. 'You know I won't tell you that. Would you answer, if I asked you that?'

He conceded the point with a slight upward jerk of the chin.

'How many members have you?'

'There's no such thing as an official membership list. The day-to-day work is handled by a group of about twenty people; but we have sympathizers all over the country, hundreds of them—some of them very highly placed.'

'Oh yes? Highly placed in what?'

'Political parties, the media, the civil

service . . .'

'Give me an example.'

There was something like contempt in Leo's gaze. 'You know I can't give you names.'

'You expect us to take a great deal on trust!'

She leaned forward. 'I came here, didn't I, when I could have been safe with my own people? What reason could I have for wanting to betray you?'

'She's right!' Margaret broke in. 'I'd still be rotting in that stinking remand centre if it wasn't for Elizabeth. How dare you question her like this!'

'I'm doing my duty!' Reilly snapped. 'I'm not going to take her on trust just because you . . .'

He broke off and Leo said quietly, 'Leave him be, Meg. He's a man. What do you expect?'

She reached out and touched the girl's hand but her eyes were on Reilly and she saw the colour rise in his neck. So that was it—good, old-fashioned jealousy!

Patrick Connor spoke for the first time, in a soft, musical voice that contrasted pleasantly with Reilly's hectoring tones.

'I'm only a man, too, but I hope you'll forgive me for speaking up. I think we should show some gratitude to Elizabeth, and her people.'

Leo caught his eye and, for a fraction of a second, she allowed her look to suggest that her opinion of his sex was not quite as low as she liked to make out.

'I simply want to know,' Reilly went on doggedly, 'who these influential people are that she claims to have working for her.'

'All right,' Leo said quietly. 'Suppose I give you a small demonstration. How would it be if tomorrow night BBC News were to show a group of my people demonstrating in favour of the "troops out" campaign?'

Patrick Connor leaned forward, his eyes fixed on her.

'Could you do that?'

She nodded.

'How?' Reilly demanded.

'By making one phone call.'

'Oh yes? Who to?'

'To our London base. It's officially a domestic service agency, but the owner, Laura Cavendish, is one of our people.'

'Just to let them know where you are, I suppose,' he commented sarcastically.

'Not at all,' she replied evenly. 'The office will be closed now. All I shall do is to dictate a message onto the Ansaphone. You can read the message beforehand and listen to me dictating it.'

Reilly hesitated. Connor said, 'Give her a chance, Kevin.'

'Show me the message,' he said abruptly.

Leo looked around her. 'Does anyone have a pen and paper?'

Stone dropped his duffel bag on the doorstep of no. 17 Daltry Road and rang the doorbell. It was answered by a small, grey-haired man in a waistcoat and bedroom slippers.

'Mr Bagley?' Stone asked.

'Ay,' he agreed.

'I was told that you sometimes let rooms. I'm looking for somewhere until I get fixed up with a place of my own.'

'And who might you be?' the little man asked suspiciously.

'My name's Smart—Paul Smart. I've just come out of the RAF and I'm looking for work. Some mates of mine think they might be able to fix me up, but I need somewhere to stay. Do you have a room?'

Bagley looked him up and down. 'Ay, well—happen I might have. You'd best come in.'

A few minutes of formal negotiation followed, and then Stone found himself in possession of the front first-floor bedroom. He put his bag on the bed and went straight to the window. Opposite, about four houses down, was the house where Leo had been taken that morning. The men from the Gas Board were just packing up. Stone reached into an inside pocket and produced his radio.

'Kappa One, this is Delta One—are you receiving me?'

'Kappa One here. Go ahead.'

'I'm in position. Any word from Theta One and Two?'

'Affirmative, Delta One. They've found a derelict factory in the next street, overlooking the rear.'

'What about Omega?'

'Still in the house. The bleeps are still coming through loud and strong.'

'Have you had visual contact?'

'Briefly, this morning. Front first-floor window.'

'OK. You'd better get on your way. Can't have the Gas Board paying you overtime!'

'See you tomorrow, then. I don't reckon we've had our money's worth out of this hole yet. Kappa One out.'

Stone took a flask and a packet of sandwiches out of his bag and settled down near the window. Of all jobs, the one he most hated was surveillance; and this one looked like going on indefinitely. Nevertheless, he had to admit to himself that he would have been a good deal more disgruntled had it not been Leonora he was keeping watch over. It bothered him that it was so long since anyone had actually seen her. The fact that the bugs were still working did not necessarily mean that she was there—or that she was alive.

Around eleven he saw the light go on in the front bedroom but the curtains had already been closed and he could not see who was in there. It was an hour later that he was finally rewarded by the sight of a pin-point of light from the window—three long flashes, the Morse code for the letter O. The signal was repeated three times and then the darkness remained unbroken.

Stone called Theta One and Two on the radio.

'I've just received the agreed recognition signal. Who's night-watchman?'

'Me, I'm afraid,' replied Theta Two. 'I'm on my way.'

A couple of minutes later an elderly Ford nosed round the corner and parked a few houses away, but no one got out of it. Stone yawned, took a last look at the window of Leo's room and turned in.

*   *   *

The following morning, in a mews not far from Harrods, Linda, junior secretary in the Cavendish Domestic Agency, played over the messages that had collected on the answering machine overnight. Then she looked into the inner office, where the manageress was checking the day's arrangements.

'Miss Parsons, there's ever such an odd message on the tape. I don't quite know what to do about it.'

'Odd?' queried Irene Parsons. 'In what way?'

'Well, for one thing, it says it's from Laura. Would that be Miss Cavendish?'

'From Laura? Yes, it must be. All right. I'll come and listen.'

The girl depressed the play button on the machine.

'I've got a message from Laura,' said the metallic, disembodied voice. 'Please contact Mr Marriot and tell him that Mr Pascoe is giving a party tonight in aid of the Troops Home Comforts Fund, and might need a bit of extra help.'

'How strange!' Irene murmured. 'Fancy Laura ringing all the way from the USA with a message like that—or rather, getting someone else to ring. I wonder who it was.'

'What do we do?' Linda asked.

'Oh, that's no problem,' Irene said briskly. 'We know how to get hold of Mr Marriot. He works for some health club in the West End but I don't think they pay him much. He sometimes does some freelance work for us— casual waiting and that sort of thing. His number's on the file.'

'Marriot?' put in Jane, the blonde senior secretary. 'Nick Marriot? Ooh, I remember him. He's a dish!' She sighed. 'Never has eyes for anyone but Laura when she's around, though; like all the rest of them.'

'Look up his number and give him the message, Linda,' Irene said. 'I suppose Miss Cavendish heard about this party and thought

68

he'd be glad of the extra money.'

'Have you heard from her lately?' Jane asked.

'I had a postcard last week. She's very optimistic about the prospects of opening a New York office.'

'No idea when she's coming back?'

'Not for several weeks, by the sound of it. She's planning to take a holiday when the negotiations are finished.'

'Some people have all the luck! What I wouldn't give to be where she is now!'

*   *   *

Nick was prowling around the communications room at Triple S headquarters when the telephone message came through. He had been willing Stone to get in touch and let him know how things were going in Birmingham. He had wanted to stay and help on the surveillance team but Pascoe had insisted that they could not risk his being seen and recognized by Donelly; so he had been given the job of co-ordinating arrangements from London. He listened to the message, thanked Irene politely and took the lift up to Pascoe's office.

'Leo's got a message through, via the agency.'

Pascoe looked pleased. 'That's encouraging. We agreed that she would make contact that way if possible, but I was afraid she wouldn't be allowed to make phone calls.'

'Well,' Nick said, handing his chief a sheet of paper, 'I hope you know what she's talking about, because it doesn't make any sense to me.'

Pascoe read the message and smiled. 'Yes, that's all right. When we were planning the operation we decided that it might be necessary to do something to convince Leo's new "friends" that her organization possesses some degree of influence. We thought perhaps a public demonstration, with media coverage. That's the "party" she's referring to, and she obviously wants it today. You'd better get to work on it.'

'I get it,' Nick grunted. 'It's a Rent-a-Mob job.'

'Not too big a mob, and predominantly female.'

'And what are we supposed to be demonstrating in aid of—or against?'

Pascoe looked at the piece of paper. 'I should have thought that was fairly obvious. 'Troops Home"—forget the comforts. A gesture of solidarity with her new allies.'

'Ah!' Nick nodded. 'Now I'm with you. I'll get on to it right away.'

He moved towards the door, hesitated and turned back.

'By the way, where do the people at the agency think their esteemed boss has gone to?'

'America—opening a new branch in New York.'

'Do any of them know what she really does?'

'Irene Parsons knows that she occasionally undertakes special assignments for one of the security services. We had to tell her that much to be sure that she'd cover for her if anyone started nosing around. She's been positively vetted, of course, and she's 100% reliable—but even she has no idea of the real situation.'

Nick nodded. 'I just wondered.' He paused. 'I bet Leo wishes she was in New York right now!'

*   *   *

The two women had spent most of the day either lying on their beds or sitting in the small back kitchen. Reilly had brought in copies of the newspapers which were all carrying the story of their escape on the front pages; and they listened to every news bulletin to follow the progress of the police hunt. There had been reports of sightings from all over the country and the police were said to be 'confident' that they would be back in custody very soon. Margaret was on edge, watching the street for signs of unusual activity, and Leo was at pains to distract her.

'Suppose that bloke in the red car remembers us,' the Irish girl said, more than

71

once. 'They could be searching this area already.'

'He wouldn't have recognized us in those wigs,' Leo said, reassuringly, wondering how she could impart her confidence in their security to the other girl without revealing the reason for it. 'And even if they narrowed the search down to this area, think of the thousands of houses around Birmingham. It would take them years to search them all.'

Margaret prowled restlessly across the room. 'I hate being cooped up like this!'

'So do I,' Leo agreed. 'But it's better than Risley, isn't it?'

The dark girl smiled suddenly. 'Sure, it's better than that sodding hole!' Then she looked contrite. 'Oh, I know. You don't like women to swear.'

'I just don't like to hear you using the same sexist vocabulary as a man,' Leo said quietly. 'Being equal doesn't mean coming down to their level.'

Margaret came over to the bed where Leo was lying and sat on the edge of it. 'Oh Beth, you put me to shame! You're so—so fine and—clear. But I tell you why this is better than Risley. At least here we can be on our own.'

She put out her hand and touched Leo's cheek. Leo lay without moving.

'Meg, I told you—right at the start.'

The other girl sighed. 'I know, I know.

We've to dedicate ourselves, save our energy . . . and what I'm thinking of is a mortal sin. But you don't believe in the immortal soul and eternal hell-fire!'

'No,' Leo said, 'but you do. We shan't know which of us is right until it's too late; but I have no intention of living my life carrying the burden of *your* guilt.'

Margaret looked away. 'Who's asking you to carry anything?'

'Nobody. I just wouldn't have any choice in the matter.'

There was a silence, then Margaret looked round and touched her hand. 'I'm sorry. I won't talk about it again.'

Leo pressed her fingers briefly and then swung her legs off the bed. 'Come on. You and I have done too much lying around lately. If we're going to be any use when the time comes we need to be fit. Does Reilly have any music, do you think?'

'Music?' Margaret repeated, following her to the door. 'What sort of music?'

It turned out that Reilly was not a musical man, but Liam Connor had a quite extensive collection of cassettes. Within minutes Reilly found himself banished from the kitchen, where the table was pushed to one side while the two girls stretched and twisted their bodies to the insistent rhythm of a disco beat. He watched from the door as Margaret panted and groaned as she strove to follow Leo's movements. Then his attention switched to Leonora herself and his eyes narrowed as he watched the elegance and suppleness of her body—a suppleness which would come only with long and regular practice.

At nine o'clock that evening they were sitting over the remains of a meal, watching the news on television. There was a lengthy report of the search for the two women, but it was clear that the police had no definite lead. There was also an item on the latest 'supergrass' trial in Northern Ireland which occasioned many muttered imprecations from around the table. As the bulletin went on it began to look as though Leonora had not been able to substantiate her claims for the influence of her organization. Then the picture switched to the Home Office. In the street outside thirty or forty women and a sprinkling of men were parading in a steady drizzle with placards bearing slogans such as— 'GET OUR SONS OUT OF ULSTER'; and 'WOMEN AGAINST MILITARY OPPRESSION'. Over the whole gathering hung a banner emblazoned with a rising sun and the words 'DAUGHTERS OF SUNRISE'. When the Home Secretary left there was a good deal of booing and catcalling and jostling with the police, though no actual violence.

When the item came to an end Patrick Connor reached out and switched off the television.

'Well, you can certainly deliver the goods, it seems,' he commented with a broad smile.

'Of course she can! How often does she have to prove it?' Margaret exclaimed fiercely.

All eyes turned to Reilly. He looked from one to the other.

'All right,' he said at length. 'Just what is it you're suggesting. If we decide to trust you, what are you aiming to do?'

Leo leaned forward, her eyes alight with a sudden intensity.

'Don't you see, we're all working for the same thing. You want freedom for your people. We want freedom for the people of *this* country too. We want an end to the old, oppressive, male-dominated regime. Oh, don't talk to me about a woman Prime Minister, who's only got where she is by beating the men at their own game! We have to pull down the whole system and start again. But to do that we have to discredit the present government and make it impossible for them to govern. That's where your aims and ours converge ...'

She spoke on, her voice urgent and persuasive, her face glowing. She had learnt early how to hold an audience, how to captivate them in a magic web of words, but she had never used the technique to better effect than she did that night. The discussion continued into the small hours, but by the time they went to bed three, at least, of her audience were hers for life.

CHAPTER FIVE

Over the next three days Daltry Street became the focus of a variety of activities. The Gas men spent another day poking around in the hole they had dug and consuming frequent mugs of tea; and when they had finished the Post Office decided to perform a similar operation a few yards further on. A newspaper seller set up a pitch at the corner and appeared every afternoon, at about the time the workmen were packing up, with the evening papers. Meanwhile, 'Paul Smart' ran into some cronies in the local pub and invited them back to his room to play cards. Before long there was a regular poker school in session. The visitors came and went very quietly and they usually brought Mr Bagley a bottle of Guinness or a packet of cigarettes, so he raised no objection.

Across the road, neighbours became used to the sound of disco music pulsing from the back kitchen, but no one had actually seen the two new residents. Up in his room, Stone bit his fingernails and resisted the temptation to go and knock on the door under some pretext, in the hope of catching a glimpse of Leo; while in London Nick raged through endless routine procedures designed, he was convinced, simply to keep him occupied.

On the Wednesday Reilly came in with a set of false documents for each of the girls, which identified Margaret as a cousin of his who had just arrived from Ireland and gave Leo yet another new identity as Mary Bland, a school-teacher recently divorced and currently unemployed.

'You might as well claim your social security,' he said tersely, 'we can't afford to keep you indefinitely.'

The next day Stone saw them emerge for the first time since they arrived. Leaving his gambling companion (in this case Theta Two) to continue the task of keeping an eye on the house and photographing anyone who went in or out, he slipped down the stairs and reached the street just in time to see them turning the corner. It was a disappointing outing, involving a long wait at the social security office and a couple of brief stops for shopping before they returned to the house; but at least he had seen Leo, and he knew she had seen him. Furthermore, she was wearing a green scarf over the auburn wig, a prearranged signal meaning 'all's well—nothing to report'.

The next evening Reilly, who had been out all afternoon, pushed his plate aside at the end of the meal, leaned his arms on the table and said,

'Right. I've got some new instructions.

77

Headquarters have decided to give you a chance to make yourself useful, Elizabeth.'

'Not before time,' Leo commented. 'Go on.'

Reilly glanced at the Connor brothers. 'You remember that quarry we reconnoitred a month or two back?' They nodded. 'There's a quarry over in North Wales,' he explained, 'where they keep explosives. Their security is pretty tight, always two armed men on duty at weekends and overnight and a couple of dogs, but I think I've seen a way of getting through it . . .'

'What do we want with explosives, for what we're going to do?' Liam Connor asked. Reilly glared at him and Leo had the impression that his brother had kicked him under the table, for he fell silent.

'What's the plan?' asked Patrick.

'The main difficulty is approaching the building where the stuff is kept without alerting the guards,' Reilly said. 'There's plenty of cover around the perimeter from trees and spoil heaps, but the building is in the middle of an open area with no cover for a hundred yards in each direction. However, there is a public footpath that skirts the edge of the site. See, here.' He spread an ordnance survey map on the table and pointed. 'It's very easy to miss it just where the new fence has been put up round the quarry, so it wouldn't be surprising for someone to lose their way.' He looked up. 'That's where you girls come in.

You'll get yourselves up like a couple of hikers. We'll drop you here,' he pointed to a road, 'and you can walk over the hills. When you get to the quarry you go to the main gate and attract the attention of the guards. Tell them you've lost the path and ask for a drink of water or something—anything to get you inside. If you use your obvious—advantages, you shouldn't have any trouble. As soon as you're inside you pull the guns you'll be carrying in your rucksacks and hold them up.'

'What about the dogs?' Leo asked.

'That's my job,' he returned. 'I'll be up on the rim of the quarry with a rifle. As soon as I see you inside I'll shoot the dogs. Then I'll get down and join you. By that time you should have the guards tied up and the keys to the building where they keep the explosives. After that it's a straightforward removals job.'

'How do we get the stuff out?' Leo asked.

'That's where you come in, Liam,' Reilly said. 'There's a forestry road, do you remember—here? You can get the car up it to within about four hundred yards of the buildings. You drop me, and then take the car round to that point. As soon as you hear me shoot the dogs start cutting the fence so we can bring the stuff through. Then come up and help us carry it to the car.'

'Right,' Liam nodded.

'What about me?' his brother asked.

'You're not coming on this one,' Reilly told

him. 'I want you to go to Gloucestershire—but I'll tell you about that later.'

Connor frowned and for a moment Leo thought he was going to argue, but he nodded and said no more.

'Right,' said Reilly. 'Let's get down to details . . .'

*　　*　　*

The following morning Stone was gazing moodily across the street and sipping a mug of coffee when he saw Leo at the window of the front bedroom. It was the first time she had shown herself except for the outing the day before, but what jerked Stone out of his morning lethargy was the fact that she was tying round her neck an amber scarf which had also been among the pack of clothes Nick had given her when she escaped from the prison van. Stone put down his mug and reached for his radio.

'Theta Two, this is Delta One. Come in please.'

'Theta Two,' came the reply. 'Go ahead.'

'I've just had a warning signal from Omega. I don't know what's going down, but I may need wheels. Can you get round here fast?'

'On my way, Delta One.'

Two minutes later the black Sierra slid to a standstill a short distance up the street, but another hour passed before the door of the house opposite opened and Leo came out with Margaret, Reilly and Liam Connor. As they got into Reilly's car Stone sauntered casually up the road and climbed into the Sierra.

'Where are we going?' asked Don Stevens, who answered to the code name of Theta Two.

'For a picnic, by the look of things,' Stone replied. 'Got your bucket and spade?'

As they nosed through the morning shopping crowds Stone switched on the receiver and smiled as it picked up the steady bleep of the homing device.

'OK. You can drop back a bit. She's carrying the bug.'

He picked up the microphone and called Theta One at the control centre which had been set up in the derelict factory.

'We're heading west at the moment. Can you send out a back-up car, just in case of emergencies? And put a helicopter on stand-by—we may need aerial surveillance. Also inform Control in London.'

'Roger, Delta Two,' Max replied. 'Kappa One and Two are on call. They'll be driving a white Capri. I'll keep in touch. Out.'

For the next couple of hours the two cars followed their electronic guide across country and into the Welsh mountains, always keeping far enough back to avoid any risk of being seen by Reilly or any of his companions. As they approached the fringes of Snowdonia the roads grew narrower and steeper and they were frequently held up by holiday-makers towing caravans and boats, roof racks piled high with camping equipment. Then, beyond Corwen, the direction-finder told them that their quarry had turned south. The B road, scarcely more than a lane, climbed through a narrow valley then dipped and twisted, following the contours of the hillside. Abruptly Stone said,

'Watch it. They've stopped.'

Don slowed the car to a crawl. After a few seconds Stone said,

'OK. They're off again, No, wait! We've got two signals now, diverging. Clever girl! She's managed to plant one of the bugs on someone else.'

'The question is,' Don commented, 'is she still in the car, or is she the one who got out?'

'No way of knowing.' Stone frowned. The car rounded a bend and passed through a plantation of larches. On the right hand side was a stile with a signpost indicating a public footpath. 'Here!' he said quickly. 'This is where they must have got out of the car.'

For a second of indecision he hesitated, then,

'Drop me here. My money's on Leo being on foot now. You stay with the car. I'll keep in touch.'

'OK.'

Don stopped the car and Stone jumped out and swung himself over the stile. The path led upwards through the larches, came out for a moment onto an open shoulder of hill and then dropped down again into another wooded area. Stone followed it at an easy pace, keeping an eye on the hand-held receiver which he had carried with him ever since Leo left Risley. He was tempted to hurry on, hoping to catch a glimpse of the person he was following. Some instinct told him it was Leonora but logic insisted that she could equally well still be in the car. It was a perfect day for a bit of fell-walking, with a clear blue sky that made you feel as though a shutter had been opened onto the infinity of space and the air, at this altitude, as sharp as a champagne bubble. Somewhere a skylark was flinging a shower of silver notes over the landscape and for a moment a cuckoo called in the next valley. Stone drew a long breath, and wished that he was walking with Leo, rather than a couple of hundred yards behind her.

*   *   *

A mile or so further on, as the car crested a rise, Reilly said,

'Drop me here. I can make my way over the hill from this point. You know where to meet me.'

There was a road junction here, and a few cottages; hardly enough to be called a village but sufficient to merit their own public call-box. Reilly watched until Liam and the car had disappeared over the rise, glanced at his watch and then entered the box and made a brief call. After that he climbed a dry-stone wall and set off briskly across the short turf, sending half a dozen sheep scuttering away over the hill. He was wearing walking boots and carried a rucksack, like any other mountain walker. The only thing that might have seemed unusual, up there, was that he also appeared to be carrying a fishing-rod.

Stone's path followed a wide curve around the shoulder of the hill. He was about to cross another stile when his radio bleeped. He sat on the top bar and answered it.

'Delta One.'

'Delta One, this is Theta Two. The car is now parked at the end of a forestry road, but our tall, dark friend isn't in it. Nor are the ladies.'

'Thank you, Theta Two. Where are you, exactly?'

Don gave him a set of co-ordinates which put him about a mile away on the far side of the hill.

'Roger, Theta Two,' Stone replied. 'Maintain observation.'

He put his radio back into his pocket and spread the map on his knee, studying the route of the path as it converged with the road which the car had taken. It was then that he saw the quarry.

For a moment or two he sat very still, studying the landscape ahead of him and listening, his mind racing. Then he got off the stile and set off at a steady jog along the path. After a short distance he came to a fence which dropped down from the hill on his left and then turned and skirted the edge of the path, which ran once again through trees at this point. Stone hesitated for a moment, then turned off the path and began to climb, following the line of the fence up through scrubby bushes and out onto the open hillside. From here he could see that, as he suspected, the fence encircled the quarry which was like a huge, semi-circular bite taken out of the hillside. The footpath lay along the bottom of it, but where he was climbing the ground rose until the rock face which being quarried dropped in a two-hundred foot cliff to the flat area where the small collection of buildings and the machinery stood, idle now for the weekend.

Stone's radio bleeped again. This time it was Viv Vivian in the Kappa Two car.

'Listen, man, I don't know if it's anything to do with us, but two car-loads of fuzz have just passed us. They're heading in your direction, and they're in a hurry.' Stone felt his guts twist themselves into a knot. Viv voiced his thoughts. 'You don't think they could have picked up Omega's trail, do you?'

'It's possible,' Stone replied, 'but God

knows how. Where are you, Kappa Two?'

'Parked in a lay-by on the main road. Theta Two followed the car up into the woods but he told us to hang back here.'

'Roger, Kappa Two. Stay where you are, and let me know if you see any further police activity. Are you in touch with Theta One at base?'

'Affirmative, Delta One.'

'What is the position regarding the chopper I asked for?'

'Standing by at RAF Towyn.'

'Tell them to scramble it. I've got a feeling we may need all the help we can get. Delta One out.'

Stone thrust the radio into his pocket and took the last hundred feet at a scrambling run, keeping low so that no one in the quarry would see him against the sky-line. When he reached the shoulder of the hill he dropped down behind an outcrop of rocks and studied the scene below him. He saw the girls at once, standing on the far side of the gates which barred the entrance, talking to two security men. The conversation was animated and, now that he was still, he could just hear Leo's voice and the familiar, mischievous laugh that had quickened his pulses so often before. It was not hard to guess what her aim was, and knowing her as he did it was impossible to believe that she would not succeed.

There was no sign of Reilly, but that was to

be expected. Stone raised his field-glasses and scanned the path on both sides of the gate, but there was plenty of cover and he was not surprised that there was nothing to be seen. Then a movement immediately below him caught his eye and sent a jolt of alarm through him. Reilly was lying on his stomach only about forty feet away, at the very edge of the cliff, watching the tableau below him and resting a rifle on a flat-topped rock.

Stone had scarcely begun to consider the implications of this discovery when his eye was again distracted, this time by a glint of sunshine on metal away on the far side of the quarry, where the road which served it led down into the valley. There, through the trees, the sun was catching the roofs of two cars, heading upwards at speed.

Stone ground his teeth. Now what? Was his prime duty to prevent Reilly from shooting the two guards, which was apparently his intention? Or was the first priority to prevent the police from recapturing Leo and bringing all their plans to nothing—and, if so, did not this mean preventing the capture of Reilly and the others, with all that that implied in terms of aiding and abetting?

While the kaleidoscope of possibilities was still forming and reforming in his head the situation changed yet again. The guards finally succumbed to Leo's blandishments and opened the gates. The two girls moved into the compound, Margaret leaning heavily on Leonora's shoulder as if unable to put her weight on one foot. As the four figures began to move towards the huts there was a sudden outburst of barking and an Alsatian appeared and bounded towards them. One of the men shouted at it and it stopped barking and contented itself with circling the little group at a distance, its belly close to the earth and its tail down.

Just below Stone, Reilly raised his rifle and sighted carefully; but as he did so two more figures appeared, climbing the slope along the opposite rim of the quarry. Stone focused his glasses and identified them as two police marksmen, also armed with rifles. His stomach contracted again as he thought of Leo caught in the centre of the arena below them, at the focal point of all this fire-power.

Reilly, intent upon his aim, had not seen the policemen. His finger tightened on the trigger and he fired once, re-aimed and fired again, the two shots following each other in rapid succession. The Alsatian leaped stiff-legged into the air, fell on its side and lay still. At the same instant the police car arrived with a scream of tyres outside the gate, which the guards had relocked behind the two girls. Four men tumbled out, two of them carrying hand guns which they aimed at the group in the centre of the quarry, and Stone heard one yell,

'Stop! Armed police!'

But Leo was already away and running like a hare towards the nearest spoil heap, dragging Margaret with her by the wrist. On the far rim of the quarry the two marksmen were searching the hillside for the source of the two shots. Stone saw Reilly jerk himself to his knees and sweep the rifle round in an arc, but it was still aimed low and, in a split second of revelation, he realized that the target was Leo. Stone flung himself full length on the grass, dragging his automatic from its holster as he did so, his arms extended, the gun in both hands. There was no time to aim; he fired by instinct and saw Reilly drop the rifle and grab at his right upper arm.

Instantaneously he rolled sideways into a steep gully behind some rocks and half slid, half scrambled, down it towards Reilly's position. He heard Reilly cursing and when he raised his head above the rocks again the Irishman was already running, bent double with his arm clasped across his body, towards the crest of the hill. One of the marksmen spotted him and Stone heard the whine as a bullet ricocheted off a rock a few yards away.

Below, in the few seconds which had passed, the girls had covered perhaps two-thirds of the distance to the cover of the spoil heap; and one of the guards was swinging open the gate to admit the police car. Stone heard the crack of a .38 and saw the earth spurt up as a bullet hit the ground just ahead of the running figures. Reilly's rifle lay where he had dropped it. Stone vaulted the ridge of rocks and grabbed it. Aiming with great care, he put a bullet into the tyre of the car as it began to advance into the compound, and then another two over the heads of the policemen. They all dived for cover and by the time they lifted their heads again the girls were among the small shrubs and loose scree around the edge of the site.

A bullet splintered the rock a foot from Stone's head. One of the marksmen had pin-pointed his position. The other was pursuing Reilly. Stone put a shot into the hillside just above the first man and saw him scramble into the cover of an outcrop of granite. As he did so Stone swung himself back into the gully and began to crawl up it as fast as he could. It took him almost to the shoulder of the hill, where the ground was broken into small patches of turf between large crags of rock. Stone dragged himself onto the top of one of these and looked back. The man who had shot at him was making his way up the slope, working from rock to rock cautiously but very steadily. Reilly and the second man had disappeared. There was no sign, either of the two girls; but Stone remembered the high, close-meshed fence which surrounded the site. They might have gone to ground for the time being, but he did not give much for their chances of getting away altogether.

In the main arena of the quarry floor men were running in all directions. The second car had arrived, and one man whom Stone guessed was the inspector in charge was standing beside it, talking on the car radio. Three men were running across the compound in the direction which Leo and Margaret had taken, while others were moving out along the line of the fence. Stone calculated he was still in range, just; but he hesitated, weighing up the desirability of slowing down the pursuit against the risk of revealing his own position again. At that moment, he heard the helicopter approaching and, twisting round, saw it moving along the valley behind him.

He steadied the rifle on the top of the rock and put a neat pattern of shots into the ground all round the three men, who scattered and threw themselves down. Within five seconds they were up and running again, but this time towards the shelter of the buildings. Stone ducked back behind his rock as the man pursuing him dropped flat and took aim, and in this temporary shelter pulled out his radio.

'Come in, Kappa One!' he said urgently.

Barney Lightfoot answered immediately. 'Kappa One here. What's going on?'

'Can't explain now,' Stone said. 'Patch me through to the chopper.'

'Roger, Delta One,' came the reply, and a few seconds later a new voice said,

'Skylark here.'

'Skylark, this is Delta One. I need a pick up. Can you see the hill to the north-west of you which has an outcrop of rocks and a single tree on the summit?'

'Affirmative, Delta One,' came the laconic reply.

'I am on the shoulder to the north. I can't risk showing myself until the last minute but I can see you. I'll talk you in until you're close enough.'

'Roger, Delta one.'

He saw the helicopter dip and twist towards the hill. Stretching up, he took a cautious look over the top of the rock. The policeman was only a hundred feet or so below him. Obviously he had heard the helicopter too, for he was searching the sky; but from his position it was hidden from him by the summit of the hill. Stone dropped back and lifted his radio to his mouth.

'Skylark, this is Delta One. Keep your present heading, but come down about a hundred feet.'

'Roger, Delta One.'

On this side the drop was much steeper, almost precipitous. The helicopter beat along, parallel to the slope, slightly above the level at which Stone was crouching in the shelter of the rock. He waited until he could see the open hatch in the side of the machine and the crewman waiting inside it, then stripped off his grey anorak.

'Skylark, you are almost level with me now. I am wearing a red shirt. Can you see me?'

A fractional pause, then,

'Got you, Delta One. Stand by.'

He saw the crewman drop a rescue harness out of the hatch. The helicopter side-slipped towards him, until the harness dangled a tantalizing ten or twelve feet away. Stone struggled back into his jacket and slung the rifle on his shoulder. He knew that the chopper must be clearly visible now to the man who was following him, and to the others in the quarry. He stood up and scrambled onto a rock which thrust itself out from the hillside over the sheer drop; and as he did so he heard a shot and saw the crewman jerk back and disappear into the interior of the machine.

'What the hell's going on down there?' crackled the voice over the radio.

'Come down another ten feet,' Stone said urgently.

The helicopter jinked and wavered as the pilot struggled to keep it steady in the cross currents of air coming over the hillside, then dropped so that the rope swung across within arm's reach. Stone made a grab into the abyss, caught it and hung on. As he did so something tore at his arm, almost making him lose his grip, and looking down he saw that a bullet had ripped the sleeve of his jacket; but already the chopper was gaining height and turning away so as to put the hilltop between itself and the marksman. Stone clung on where he was until they were out of range; then felt himself being winched up into the cabin.

CHAPTER SIX

It was not the arrival of the police car which started Leo running, nor the shot which killed the dog. It was Reilly's second shot, the wind of which lashed across her cheek before it thudded into the ground behind her. If she had not turned at that instant, her attention attracted by the arrival of the car, the bullet would certainly have ended in her brain.

There was no time, however, for speculations of this nature as she raced towards the shelter of the nearest spoil heap. She was only aware of gunfire from all around, none of which mercifully seemed aimed at her. She could hear Margaret sobbing for breath behind her and reflected grimly that it was a pity she had not started her keep-fit campaign earlier. They slipped and scrambled over the loose shale at the base of the heap and paused for a second once they were out of sight. Ahead of them the fence stretched unbroken in both directions. Leo felt a sudden, sickening sense of hopelessness. The she spotted a line of grass and tall, rank weeks which skirted the base of the mound and ran towards the fence, stopped for a few feet and then reappeared on the far side.

'Come on!' she shouted to Margaret.

They ran headlong down the slope and half jumped, half fell, into the ditch which was marked by the line of weeds. In the bottom of it was a few inches of muddy water, but on both sides the nettles and cow-parsley grew to a height of three or four feet. Leo squirmed forward on her stomach until the weeds formed an unbroken canopy above her head and then lay still, listening and trying to control her laboured breathing. Behind her she could hear Margaret panting, but for a few minutes there was no sound of pursuit. Then heavy feet tramped along the stony ground beside the fence, passing within yards of where they lay. They heard the men shouting to each other, and then one called,

'Hey Sarge, the fence had been cut up here. They must have gone this way.'

Leo caught her breath. Liam Connor had done his part of the job before the balloon went up and unwittingly laid a false trail to lead the police away from them. She twisted round and whispered,

'Come on.'

Keeping flat on their bellies the two girls inched along the ditch, gritting their teeth as nettle stings burned every exposed inch of skin and brambles tore at their clothes. Soon Leo saw ahead of her what she had guessed at from the slope above; the stream ran through a culvert which passed under the fence. The pipe which carried it was about three feet in diameter and perhaps six long. Leo wriggled into it and then turned her head and hissed to Margaret,

'Squeeze in here beside me. We'll have to lie low until the heat's off.'

After some scrabbling and struggling Margaret succeeded in hauling herself in beside Leo so that they lay pressed together in the trickle of muddy water which flowed through the pipe. It was at that point that they first heard the helicopter. Margaret whispered,

'Mother of God, now we'll never get away.'

'Yes, we will,' Leo told her. 'That forestry plantation out there is perfect cover. Once we're in there they'll never spot us from the air.'

They listened as the sound of the machine grew closer, and heard the shouts of the men searching for them move away in that direction. Then the noise of the engine faded again and in the quiet which followed Leo heard a blackbird chuntering to itself in the undergrowth beyond the end of the culvert. She eased herself forward, whispering,

'Stay here while I have a look.'

Peering up through the weeds she could see no sign of their pursuers. The ditch crossed a narrow band of open ground and then disappeared into a dense plantation of firs.

Leo hissed,

'Wait till I get into the trees, then if there's still no sign of anyone follow me.'

Keeping low, in a shambling movement that was half crawl, half run, Leo crossed the space between the fence and the forest and dragged herself out of the ditch under the low-growing branches of the firs. A minute later Margaret joined her and, without further speech, Leo lead the way deeper into the wood. Their progress was slow and difficult since the trees grew so close together and so low to the ground that they either had to force their way through the sharp-twigged, leafless branches which sprouted from the lower part of the trunks, or else get down and crawl under them.

Eventually they came to the edge of a narrow road which slanted up the hill more or less at right angles to their line of progress. Margaret said,

'This must be the road Liam was going to take. I remember it from the last time we came.'

'Well, that doesn't help us any, I'm afraid,' Leo remarked. 'Either Liam must be miles away by now, or the police have got him.'

Margaret leaned against a tree trunk.

'What do we do now, then?'

'Keep going,' Leo told her. 'Our biggest danger is dogs. I don't mind betting they're on their way already. So we have to find water.'

She reached into the rucksack which she

still carried on her back and found the map which Reilly had given her that morning.

'There's a small valley ahead which comes down to join the main one where the road is, and there's a stream marked. We'll head for that.'

They darted across the road and into the trees again on the far side. After a while the ground began to slope more steeply and the plantation of firs ended, to be replaced by a more natural growth of small oaks and silver birch. They scrambled down the last steep bank and found themselves on the edge of a small, fast-flowing stream which tumbled down a narrow ravine. Leo stepped into the water and turned upstream.

'Not that way!' Margaret exclaimed. 'The road's down there.'

'And so are the police!' Leo said tersely. 'That's the way they will expect us to go. Come on.'

The water was only just over ankle deep but it was icy-cold and the bed of the stream was rocky and very treacherous. They struggled upwards, often slipping and sometimes hauling themselves up with their hands as the gradient grew steeper. Before long they were both soaked from head to foot. Eventually the slope grew less and the walls of the ravine opened out until they stood at the head of a rounded depression, like a giant thumb-print on the shoulder of the mountain. Leo squatted down in the lee of a large rock and Margaret flung herself on the ground beside her. Neither of them spoke; they had no energy left for words, but after a moment Leo once more pulled out the map and began to study the landscape around them.

To their right a long grassy slope dropped away in gentle folds and undulations towards the valley, where she could pick out the roofs of two groups of houses and the occasional flash of reflected light from the bodywork of cars moving along the road which connected them. She glanced at the map, estimating the distance—a couple of hours easy walking, perhaps. To their left the ground rose steeply to the sharp ridge which joined the line of rocky peaks dividing this valley from the next; but ahead of them, perhaps three or four hundred feet above their present position, was a saddle, a depression between two mountains, which offered a possible route by which the ridge might be crossed. The first part of the climb was simply an upwards slog over rough pasture, with enough rocks and gullies to give cover if the helicopter came back. The last hundred feet or so looked much steeper, but from where they sat it did not appear to Leo to present any real problems in terms of actual rock climbing.

She looked down at her companion, prostrate on the grass, and then at her watch. It was a little after four. There was plenty of daylight left but at this altitude there was little warmth left in the sunlight. If they spent too much longer on the mountain in their wet clothes she knew that they both ran the risk of hypothermia. The obvious answer was to head for the friendly rooftops of one of the villages; but equally obviously that was going to be one of the first places the police would look for them. On the other hand, the far valley was so cut off by the mountain ridge, the nearest connecting road being some eight miles further on, that they would hardly expect to find them there. The question was, could Margaret make the climb? It would be better to be picked up by the police than to be caught on the mountain with night coming down and the Irish girl in a state of collapse. Once again Leo's thoughts turned to Stone. What were the chances of his finding them before the police did? She put her hand to her head and only then became aware that the auburn wig had gone, snatched off, presumably, when they were wriggling along the ditch. The stud from her jeans pocket had been left behind long ago, wedged down the back of the car seat to give Stone and his team a chance to follow the car as well. There was no hope, then, from that quarter. She felt herself beginning to shiver and stood up.

'Come on, Meg.'

The girl raised her head. 'How much further?'

'We've got a bit more climbing to do,' Leo told her briskly. 'Then, once we're over the other side, we'll look for somewhere warm to hide up for the night.'

'Over where?' Margaret asked, her eyes wandering across the hillside. The she saw the saddle. 'Dear God! We're never going right up there!'

'Come on,' repeated Leo, beginning to move away. 'It's not as far as it looks.'

It was—and further! For two hours they toiled upwards, scarcely speaking, the rough ground unbalancing them and preventing them from settling into a steady stride. Twice they took cover under the shadow of rocks as a helicopter flew backwards and forwards along the hillside. It was a police helicopter, but, as Leo had guessed, it was obviously concentrating on the lower slopes. By the time they reached the steep escarpment of rock and scree immediately below the saddle Margaret was giving a low, moaning sob on every outward breath and Leo could see that she was almost at the end of her strength. She undid the scarf which she had knotted around her neck as a sign to Stone, folded it into a strip and gave one end to the other girl.

'Hang on. I'll help you up.'

Step by step, Leo worked her way up the slope, picking out each ledge of rock to stand on and each tuft of grass to cling to, and then half dragging the exhausted Margaret after her. Long before they reached the top Leo, too, was at the end of her strength and only the knowledge that to stop now would mean almost certain death from exposure for them both kept her going. Finally, every muscle in her body shuddering under the strain, she hauled herself onto the level turf of the saddle and lay gasping, aware only of the blood thundering in her ears.

The chill of the evening breeze roused her to the awareness that they were far from safe yet. She struggled to her knees and looked down the valley before her. The slope on this side, thank God, was easier and a hundred feet or so below was a wooded gully with what looked like a path leading into it; and further down still there were the roofs of some buildings. Leo turned and put her hand on Margaret's shoulder.

'Just a short walk down hill, Meg. Then we'll find somewhere to shelter.'

Margaret lifted her face, streaked with mud and tears.

'Mother of God, I can't walk another step!'

'Margaret,' Leo said urgently, 'if you stay here you will die. I'm not just saying that to get you on your feet. It's true. You're wet and exhausted and cold. You wouldn't survive a night up here.'

Slowly Margaret sat up, rubbing her face on her sleeve.

'This is a fearsome place! How is it you

know so much about it? Aren't you terrified too?'

Leo smiled at her. 'No, not now. I know we can make it down to safety now. Just one more effort, that's all it needs.'

'But where did you learn to find your way around in a wilderness like this?' the girl insisted.

'Oh,' Leo looked away, across the shadowy hills. 'I've always liked the solitary places. But what about you? You have your own mountains in Ireland.'

'Oh, not for me!' Margaret shivered. 'Give me the city streets any day.'

'Even when there's a sniper at every corner?' Leo murmured. She rose to her feet. 'Come on. This is no place to rest.'

As she strode forward down the slope it occurred to her that for the last couple of hours she had almost forgotten that the girl following in her footsteps was a self-confessed killer who had shot a man in cold blood only a few weeks ago.

Once they reached the path the going was easier and after a mile or so they found themselves on a rough track which wound down a wooded valley. Rounding a bend they came in sight of a small, stone-built cottage standing in a neat garden. Leo stopped and moved into the shadow of the trees. The cottage had obviously been built as a farmworker's home but now the new, oak front door and the freshly painted window-frames suggested a week-end retreat. All the windows were shut and there was no sign of light or movement behind them.

'Empty, d'you reckon?' Margaret asked.

'No car,' Leo said, 'and no garage to hide one in. They'd need transport up here, so that suggests there's no one at home right now. Of course, they could just have gone down to the pub . . .'

She paused, studying the house. It didn't look occupied . . .

'Wait here,' she instructed Margaret. 'I'll check it out.'

Margaret slumped down on the grass with her back against a tree trunk, while Leo stepped out onto the track and plodded towards the cottage, as unconcerned as any weary hiker at the end of a long walk. When she reached the gate she paused, looking up the path. There was still no sign of life from inside. Without any attempt at concealment she walked up the path and knocked at the front door. When she had knocked three times without any response she wandered casually around to the back of the house. All the ground-floor rooms were unoccupied and in the lounge the chair cushions were uncreased and the ashtrays empty.

Having finished her inspection Leo looked around the garden. In a shed she found exactly what she wanted—a small spade. Armed with this she returned to the kitchen window and after a couple of minutes judicious manipulation succeeded in joggling the catch of the small top window off its pin. From there it was simple to reach in and open the larger window and within seconds she was standing in the kitchen. Another brief search produced a pair of rubber gloves from the drawer under the draining-board and, once she had put these on, she turned her attention to wiping her fingerprints off the handle of the spade, the window catch and anything else she might have touched, reflecting grimly as she did so that having acquired a police record had disadvantages which had not previously struck her. Finally she made a rapid tour of the house. There was no milk in the fridge, no clothes in the cupboards, the beds were not made up. Unless they were very unlucky and the owners were planning to arrive that night, they were safe—at least for the time being.

Leo opened the front door and called softly to Margaret and a few seconds later the other girl stumbled through the hallway and threw herself onto the settee in the living-room. Leo, who had taken her boots off in the kitchen, regarded the trail of muddy footprints and the damp, dirty figure at the end of it grimly for a moment; then drew a long breath and padded upstairs in search of blankets.

*   *   *

Stone called up Kappa One and Two from the helicopter and arranged a rendezvous where a minor road crossed a remote upland pasture a couple of valleys away. When the helicopter had dropped him and sped on its way to get the injured crewman into hospital he crouched down in the shelter of a stone sheep-fold and took out the direction-finder which was tuned to the transmitters Leo had been given. There was no signal from either of the two bugs and he swore under his breath at the implications.

Barney and Viv Vivian arrived ten minutes later and Stone's first words as he climbed into the back of the Capri were,

'Have you still got a trace on Omega?'

''Fraid not,' said Viv. 'One's gone out of range, the other one stopped transmitting soon after you called up the chopper.'

'Hell!' said Stone. 'That's the one she was carrying.'

'What's been going on, anyway?' Barney asked. 'You seem to have started your own private war.'

Stone told them briefly what had happened in the quarry.

'You say the bug in the car's gone out of range?' he added. 'They got away, then?'

Barney nodded. 'Don's gone after them. They took off even before we lost the other trace. Looks like they didn't even wait to see if the girls made it.'

'That figures,' Stone said grimly. 'I reckon Reilly set the whole thing up, anyway.'

'What the hell for?' Viv asked.

'To get rid of Leo. He tried to shoot her twice. The first time I thought I could be mistaken, but the second there was no question about. My guess is he tipped off the police, then planned to start the shooting as soon as they arrived, knowing they would respond, and make it look as though Leo had been caught in the cross-fire.'

'And killed by a police bullet?' Barney suggested.

Stone looked at the Armalite beside him on the seat. 'That's what he was using. Same type as the standard police issue. Forensic would have shown that the bullet hadn't come from one of the police weapons, of course, but I doubt if Reilly's people would have believed that.'

'I don't get it,' objected Viv. 'What about the other girl?'

'Presumably he would have let the police retake her.'

'One of his own people?' Viv was scandalized.

Stone shrugged. 'Looked at from his point of view he was perfectly right, of course. Donelly had endangered his whole operation by taking Leo to the house. He had to get rid of Leo, and he had to make sure she didn't have a chance to talk. He could have shot her in cold blood and dumped her body in the canal, of course, but my guess is the rest of the group wouldn't go along with that, so he had to make it look as if the police had shot her. If that meant shopping Donelly too, well, as commander of a unit in the field, he had to sacrifice one person for the good of the group.'

'Cold-blooded sod!' commented Viv.

'Maybe,' Stone said. 'Anyway, he didn't succeed and now it looks as if he's buggered off back to Brum and left them to fend for themselves. The only question now is, who finds them first—us or the police.' He paused, then added, 'That is, if they haven't picked them up already.'

'Doesn't look like it,' said Barney. 'They're setting up road-blocks. We came through one on the way up here.'

Stone's face brightened. 'Good. They must have got clear for the time being, at any rate.'

'So where do we start looking?' Viv asked, gazing out at the empty moorland around them.

'Well, the first thing, obviously, is to get back to somewhere near the quarry where we can see what the police are up to. They're bound to have brought in dogs by now. If they've picked up a trail it might give us a clue where to start. Other than that—'he compressed his lips and lifted his shoulders slightly—'there's no point in us three trying to comb an area like that on spec. The best thing we can do is to try and let Leo know where we are and hope she'll find us.' He glanced at his watch. 'My bet is that they'll look for somewhere to hole up for the night and then hope to slip past the road-blocks in the morning; but sooner or later they're going to need transport and that means coming back to the road. Leo would recognize this car, being one of the pool cars, and she knows you two. All we can do for now is patrol the roads around the area and hope she'll spot us and make contact.'

'What's with all this "we" bit?' Viv asked. 'You're a wanted man.'

'Viv's right,' Barney said. 'After that little run-in with the local boys you ought to be keeping your head down. Did any of them get a good look at you?'

Stone's jaw tightened. 'Yes, I guess the guy with the rifle must have done. But they won't be looking for me round here.'

'Just the same,' Barney said, 'trying to drive through police check-points is putting your head in the lion's mouth. You leave this to us.'

'What's your cover story, anyway?' Stone asked.

Viv grinned. 'Oh, don't you worry about us, man. We're just a couple of city boys out for a weekend's fishing.'

Stone raised his eyebrows. 'Without rods or tackle?'

Viv looked injured. 'You take a look in the

boot sometime. You'll find rods, lines, tackle boxes—even bait.'

'Sorry!' Stone smiled briefly. 'I should have known better.'

Barney and Viv had been with Triple S almost as long as he had, and one thing all Pascoe's agents were trained to be meticulous about was ensuring that their cover stories would stand up to close investigation.

'So if anyone asks, we're off to do a bit of night fishing,' Barney said.

'OK,' Stone gave way reluctantly. 'Drop me off somewhere where I can set up base—and keep in touch.'

'There was a pub a couple of miles back,' Barney said, 'this side of the road-block, advertising bed and breakfast. The Druid's something . . .'

'The Druid's Rest,' Viv supplied.

'That'll do,' Stone said. 'Drop me there.'

'I still don't like it,' Barney protested. 'You ought to get right out of the area.'

'Look,' said Stone, 'they saw me whisked off in a helicopter, didn't they? They're not going to be looking for me on their own back doorstep. Anyway, I'm not going anywhere until we locate Leo, so you can forget that idea.'

'OK,' said Barney unwillingly. 'The Druid's Rest it is.'

'Listen,' Stone said as Barney started the engine. 'Is this car fitted with a scrambler? I

110

need to talk to Pascoe.'

Viv passed him the handset and punched in the number. 'Help yourself.'

He got through to Pascoe without difficulty and told him what had happened in the quarry. When he finished Pascoe said,

'Right. I want you to keep your head down. Let Kappa One and Two do the searching. I'll send Marriot up to you straight away. If you succeed in locating Omega I want him to be the one to make contact. Quite apart from the fact that if the police pick you up and identify you our whole story goes down the drain, Donelly may have seen you in Daltry Road and if you turn up there in the middle of Wales she's bound to smell a rat. She knows Marriot as one of Omega's people.'

'But how's he supposed to know where they are?' Stone asked.

'There will be a report in the next radio news bulletin. I'll see to that if the BBC's bloodhounds haven't picked it up already.'

'The police may not have connected the two girls in the quarry with Donelly and "Walker",' Stone pointed out.

'Well, if necessary, we shall have to make the connection for them,' Pascoe said. 'Now, give me the precise location of this inn where you're going to stay. Marriot should be with you before midnight.'

*   *   *

111

By the time darkness came Leo and Margaret were sitting in front of an electric fire, huddled in blankets, while their damp clothes steamed gently over the backs of a couple of chairs. The kitchen cupboards had proved to be well stocked with emergency rations and with a tin of mince, another of beans, some rice and the contents of the spice rack Leo had concocted a very palatable chilli con carne. Margaret ate ravenously, but her eyes widened in disbelief when Leo insisted that they wash up afterwards.

'Let them do it!' she said. 'If they've got nothing better to do than lounge around here at weekends they can find time to wash up after us.'

'Listen,' Leo said, 'breaking into people's houses and stealing their food isn't my style, believe it or not. The least we can do is leave it tidy.'

Margaret's eyes narrowed. 'Bloody funny revolutionary, you are!'

'Besides which,' Leo continued, 'by tomorrow at the latest the police are going to be searching places like this. The best we can hope for is that I was right and they'll start the search on the other side of the mountain, so we'll be long gone before they get here. But there's no point in making it obvious to anyone glancing through the window that someone had been camping out here—to say nothing of leaving our fingerprints all over everything we've touched.'

Margaret saw sense then, and even agreed to clean up the trail of muddy footprints across the carpet. Finally, when everything was tidy and they were settled in front of the fire, she said,

'What now?'

'Now,' Leo replied, 'we take it in turns to sleep. I'll take first watch; but before that I'm going to make one phone call.'

Margaret's eyelids, which had been drooping, jerked open.

'Who to?'

'Don't worry,' Leo reassured her. 'it's to the same number I called the other day. If we're going to get out of here we need wheels. I'll leave a message for Nick Marriot on the agency tape. If they contact him first thing in the morning he could be here by lunch time.'

'I don't like it.' Margaret frowned at her beneath the heavy fringe of dark hair. 'I don't like involving other people.'

'Listen!' Leo's voice had an edge to it. 'Marriot got us out of Risley. Your people are going to be no good to us. I bet Reilly and Liam are safely back in Birmingham by now.'

'How do you know? Kevin could be out there now, looking for us.'

'Yeah?' Leo said sceptically.

'Why not?'

'Has it occurred to you to wonder how it

was that the police turned up just at that precise moment?' Leo asked.

'Of course it has. I don't know how they knew.'

'There's only one possible explanation. Someone shopped us—and only Reilly and the Connors knew about it, apart from us.'

Margaret stared at her. 'I don't believe it. None of them would have talked—unless . . . That Liam Connor likes a drink. If he's blabbed his mouth off in a pub somewhere . . .'

Leo watched her with narrowed eyes. Her disbelief seemed genuine.

'Well,' she said eventually, 'I think I prefer to trust my own people at the moment.'

She found the map and studied it for a few moments, then went to the telephone and dialled the number of the Cavendish Agency. When the recorded message had finished and the tone indicated that the machine was ready she said, in a voice with just a hint of an American accent,

'This is Elizabeth, Laura's friend. I called the other day? I'm sorry to bother you like this, but I arranged to meet your Nick Marriot today and he hasn't turned up. I'm stuck here in the middle of Wales and I don't know his number. Could you please call his office, or wherever he works, for me and give him a message? Tell him I'll be outside the pub on the outskirts of a village called Gwytherin between two-thirty and three-thirty tomorrow afternoon. I'm really sorry to be a nuisance, but I'd be very grateful if you could do that for me. Goodbye—and thank you.'

*　　　*　　　*

Nick Marriot reached the Druid's Rest, as Pascoe had predicted, shortly before midnight. He was driving a Mini van emblazoned with the title British Conservation Trust; an organization which, like all those invented by Pascoe to cover Triple S operations, was provided with impeccable credentials. Stone grinned as they met and nodded towards the van.

'What are we on tonight then?'

'I thought badgers,' Nick returned. 'They're nocturnal.'

'Badgers . . .' Stone repeated, pursing his lips thoughtfully. 'They're the big black and white jobs, aren't they? Or am I thinking of pandas?'

'Not a lot of pandas in North Wales,' Nick told him. 'I think we'd better stick to badgers.'

Stone had booked two adjoining rooms for them, and prudently stocked his with beer and sandwiches before the bar closed. They settled down to these with the map spread between them.

'What's the situation at the moment?' Nick asked.

115

'Barney called in about two hours ago,' Stone told him. 'They managed to get up on the hill above the quarry where they had a pretty good view. The place is still crawling with police—or was at that time—and they've brought in dogs, as we expected. Barney said they seemed to be concentrating on this area, north-east of the quarry—which is reasonable because that's the direction Leo was headed last time I saw her—but, they didn't appear to have picked up a definite trail. If you look at the map you'll see why, probably . . .'

Nick leaned over the map. 'Yes, I see. A stream. Of course, Leo would make for water. The question is, which way did she go—up or down?'

'Well, the obvious way would be down.'

'So Leo will have gone up.'

Nick looked up and caught Stone's eye and they both grinned.

'OK,' Stone went on. 'Assuming she followed the stream up as far as she could that would have brought her to here.' His finger indicated a point on the map. 'You can see from the contours, this ridge is pretty steep and, having flown over it this afternoon, I can tell you they wouldn't get up there without ropes and all the rest of the gear. They could have headed downhill and taken shelter in an isolated building somewhere along this valley. There must be plenty to choose from. But there is one other possibility. You see here?

116

There's a saddle which they could have crossed to get into the next valley. It would be a tough climb. but not impossible. The question is, which did they do?'

Once again Nick met his eyes. 'You're asking me if they took the easy option or the difficult one? We're talking about Leo, remember?'

Stone laughed briefly. 'OK. So we're both thinking along the same lines. But what about the other girl? You've seen her. Did she look the mountaineering type to you?'

Nick pursed his lips and shook his head. 'Little short legs and a pasty complexion— more your Pekinese than your wolfhound, if you get me. However, having said that, from what I saw I'd take odds that if Leo told her to shin up the side of a house, she'd have a go.'

Stone nodded. 'I agree. So we start looking on that side of the mountain.'

'*I* start looking,' Nick corrected him. 'Strict orders from Pascoe. You're to stay out of sight.'

'Bloody hell!' Stone exploded. 'What am I supposed to do?'

'Get your head down and have a sleep, I should think,' Nick suggested reasonably.

Stone glowered at him. 'And if you find her . . . ?'

'I'll give her your love, shall I?'

Stone knew that Pascoe's decision was the correct one and that it was useless to argue, but he saw Nick off with a bad grace. Barney called in on the radio soon afterwards. He and Viv had combed the roads in the area without seeing any sign of the two girls, and had attempted to follow the stream where the police were searching, under the pretext of looking for a likely trout pool, but had been turned back. They had decided that there was nothing more to be done that night and found themselves bed and breakfast at a farmhouse. After that there was nothing he could do either so he turned in and dozed fitfully until the birds woke him around 5 a.m.

Nick returned just after six, looking weary and cold. He, too, had had a fruitless night, enlivened only by an encounter with a helpful constable of naturalist leanings who had wished to give him a conducted tour of every badger set in the vicinity.

After breakfast they went out to the van and called Triple S HQ on the scrambler. Pascoe came on the line very quickly.

'I've been waiting for you to call. The Cavendish Agency have been in touch. Omega left a message for you on their answering service sometime last night . . .'

*　　　*　　　*

The two women left the cottage at first light on a day which had dawned grey and overcast, with rain threatening. During one of her spells

118

on watch, Leo, prowling around the house, had found some coats in a cupboard and, after a brief struggle with her conscience, had 'borrowed' two anoraks. With these zipped to the chin and the hoods drawn close around their faces they were not only protected from the weather, they were also very much less easily recognizable. After a short distance Leo led the way off the track and struck out for a band of trees which ran along the side of the hill for several miles. There was no path and, once again, they found themselves having to force their way through dense undergrowth and climb over fences and dry stone walls but Gwytherin was only just over six miles distant and by midday they were crouching under the shelter of the downward-sweeping branches of an ancient yew, looking down at the outskirts of the village.

Several times during the morning the police helicopter had beat up and down the valley, while they froze under the sheltering trees; and now, watching the road, they could see police cars moving backwards and forwards, but there was no sign of the lines of men sweeping the countryside which Leo had feared. They shared a packet of biscuits which they had brought from the cottage, and waited. A little after two Leo began to search for a vantage-point from which she could see the car-park in front of the little inn. The roof of the inn itself was clearly distinguishable and they had seen people coming and going over the lunchtime opening period but the car-park itself was hidden. In the end she found that the only way to see it was by clambering up into the branches of the yew, and it was from here that she saw the Conservation Trust van drive in and pull up.

*　　　*　　　*

Nick parked the van and looked around. The car-park was deserted, but he had not expected to find the girls waiting for him. He got out, stretching himself, and gazed casually about him. The main part of the village was hidden from him by a bend in the road, along which cars passed frequently. To one side of the inn a narrow lane ran back towards the hillside, bordered by a few cottages. The rain had settled to a steady, fine drizzle and, apart from a young man stoically sawing logs in the garden of one of the cottages, there was no one about. He reached into the van and drew out a map and a pair of field-glasses and began to study the hills around section by section, as if planning the next phase of his survey. He could still see no sign of Leo and her companion, but once again, that did not unduly surprise him.

It was the coloured anoraks that caught his eye, as two weary hikers came trudging down the lane, and it was a moment or two before he could be sure that it was Leo. The man in the cottage garden looked up and gave them a cheerful good-afternoon and he heard her reply in an accent that would have located her origins in upper-class Edinburgh. He walked over to meet them and was touched by the evidences of prolonged strain on Leo's face. When, he wondered, had she last had a really good night's sleep? However, this time he was prepared for the unsmiling greeting.

'You're here. Good,' she said curtly.

'Yes,' he returned. 'Let's get going, shall we?'

'Hallo there!' a cheerful voice hailed them from the other side of the road. 'How are the badgers?'

Nick swung round and his stomach churned at the sight of the police car parked opposite. The driver in the process of climbing out was his nature-loving friend from the previous night.

Behind him Nick heard a sudden movement and Leo said, very softly between her teeth, *'Stay still!'* and he guessed that Margaret had been about to bolt. He went forward to meet the constable.

'Hallo! Fine, thanks. You were quite right, there were two sets at the head of that valley.' (He hoped to God there were—or that the copper didn't know for certain, either.)

'Oh, that's great! And a litter in both of them?'

'Yes. All doing fine.'

'Did you find any others?'

'Oh yes. Quite an encouraging night, really.'

'How many?'

'Six, altogether.' (Was that about right? How numerous were badgers in this part of the world?)

'Oh, that's good news. I don't suppose you'd tell me where the others are?'

Nick smiled apologetically. 'Sorry—regulations, you know. We're not supposed to tell anyone—even the police. That is,' he laughed, 'not unless you suspect them of receiving stolen goods or something.'

The copper laughed too. 'No, no. Not so far as I know.'

Nick saw his eyes go past him to the two girls and turned casually.

'Oh, by the way, these are my two assistants—Miss Kendall and Miss Ferguson.'

'Ah, so you don't have to do all the work by yourself,' the policeman said. 'Good-afternoon, ladies.'

Nick prayed that Margaret would have the sense to keep her mouth shut. She nodded and Leo said, in what she called her Jean Brodie voice,

'Oh, it would be far too great an area for one person to cover alone.'

'Talking of which,' Nick put in, 'how's your hunt going? Any luck yet?'

'Not so far, but it's only a matter of time.

We're checking all the empty holiday cottages. We reckon they may be hiding out in one of them. By the way, I suppose you didn't happen to see anything unusual during the night, did you? Anyone moving about, or a light in an isolated building?'

They consulted each other's eyes and shook their heads.

'Sorry,' Nick said. 'Wish we could help.'

'Oh, not to worry. We'll pick them up before long,' the copper said, cheerfully.

'You're not only just going off watch, are you?' Nick asked.

'No, just going back on, actually. What about you?'

'Oh, we've finished around here,' Nick said. 'Just about to move on to our next base.'

'Fresh fields and pastures new, eh? Well, don't let me keep you. I must be on my way too. All the best, then.' He nodded at Leo and Margaret. 'Goodbye.'

'Goodbye, Constable,' Leo replied demurely.

They watched him climb into the car and waved as he drove off. When the car was out of sight Margaret whispered,

'Mother of God!'

Leo's lips twisted for a moment into her irrepressible grin.

'Poor man! I hope he never finds out how close he was!'

'Come on,' Nick said. 'Let's get out of here.

Where did you spend the night?'

Leo jerked her head in the direction the police car had gone.

'Like the man said, in an empty holiday cottage.'

'Did you leave any signs that you'd been there?'

She treated him to a withering look that was only partly acted.

'Do me a favour! The only people who'd know would be the owners.'

'Well, let's pray the owners haven't chosen today to pay the place a visit.' Nick said. 'Get in.'

The women climbed into the back of the van, which was cluttered with a variety of equipment, including one or two shapeless heaps covered with some old blankets.

'There's a police road-block about four miles further on,' Nick told them. 'If they look like checking the back I'll bang on the partition. Be ready to get under those blankets. OK?'

They settled themselves on the floor and he climbed into the driving seat and started the engine. The check-point was one he had passed through the night before and he hoped that there might be someone on duty who remembered him. As they approached he saw a small queue of cars, mostly holiday-makers out for the day, ahead of him. The police check seemed fairly cursory, just a quick

124

glance into the car and a few questions; but as he edged nearer to the front of the line Nick felt his palms beginning to sweat and was suddenly angry at the whole situation. Here he was, an ex-copper himself, sweating with fear in spite of the fact that he was still working for the forces of law and order. But how did you convince a policeman of that if you were found aiding and abetting the escape of two prisoners, both accused of murder and now suspected of armed robbery as well? He remembered Pascoe's warning—'this one is strictly a YOYO'—and felt his mouth go dry.

'Hallo, sir. Still at it?' inquired the constable at the window.

'Just finished,' Nick said. 'Moving on now.'

'You haven't picked up any hitch-hikers by any chance?'

'Hitch-hikers?' Nick looked around at the empty seat beside him. 'No. Not much room for them really.'

'Have you see anyone hitching—two women, in particular?'

'No, sorry.'

'Righto, sir. Sorry to detain you.'

The man stood back and Nick let in the clutch and resisted the temptation to accelerate too fast. When they were well clear he reached for his microphone and said, keeping his voice low so that the Donelly girl would not hear,

'Delta One, this is Delta Two. I have

collected the parcels. Heading west on the A548.'

Stone's voice came back over the loudspeaker.

'Well done, Delta Two. We'll pick you up a couple of miles further on and check your tail. Delta One out.'

A few minutes later Nick saw the white Capri in his rear-view mirror. It stayed with him for a few miles and then Stone's voice came over the radio again.

'Delta Two, this is Delta One. You're clean, as far as we can tell. We'll drop out of sight now and monitor you on the direction-finder. OK?'

'Roger, Delta One,' Nick replied. 'Delta Two out.'

He saw the Capri turn off at the next junction and drove on for another ten miles before pulling into a lay-by and going round to open the rear doors. Leo climbed out, stretching herself, but Margaret remained hunched up on the blankets, apparently half asleep.

'Well,' Nick said. 'we're clear. What now?'

Leo glanced back into the van. 'I'll come in front and direct you. Will you be OK there for a bit, Meg?'

Meg nodded drowsily. Nick had the impression that she was too tired to care. Leo walked round and got into the front of the van and Nick took his place beside her.

For a moment they looked at each other in silence; then he leaned forward and kissed her softly. She leaned against him and he held her and rubbed his face in her hair. As she drew back he looked at her and asked,

'Are you all right?'

She smiled at him, the bitter-sweet, slightly mocking smile that always made his heart turn over.

'Yes. I'm all right.'

Reluctantly he turned away and started the engine. As he pulled out onto the road he said,

'Are we going home?'

She sighed and shook her head. ' 'Fraid not, sweetheart.'

He put his hand in his pocket and drew out a small object about the size of a button.

'In that case, you'd better have this. You seem to have been rather careless with the last two I gave you!'

*   *   *

'You dropped her where?'

Stone was a cool man, some people who didn't know him well would have said a cold man. He rarely showed emotion, still less often lost his temper, but at that moment all the anxiety and frustration of the last twenty-four hours vented themselves on Nick. They had arranged a rendezvous by radio and now they were sitting in the van in another deserted pub car-park.

'Look!' Nick said, in a gritty tone that matched his partner's. 'Pascoe told me to be guided by Leo's decision. And Leo was determined to go back to Daltry Road.'

'You idiot!' Stone snapped. 'Of all the bloody stupid, incompetent . . . Reilly tried to shoot her! And you've let her walk straight back into his hands!'

Nick's face paled. 'You didn't tell me that!'

'I told Pascoe, on the phone. You said he'd briefed you.'

'He did, but he never mentioned that. All he said was, if Leo wants to come out, then ditch Donelly and bring her back here; but if she feels that she can carry on, let her—at least then we shan't have to abort the whole operation.'

'Typical!' Stone exclaimed. 'Bloody typical! Never mind what happens to Leo, as long as the operation goes ahead. God, sometimes I hate that bastard!'

'I don't think that's entirely fair,' Nick put in quietly. 'But it's true he didn't tell me the whole story. When did Reilly try to shoot her?'

Stone told him what he had seen in the quarry.

'Do you think it's possible that Leo didn't realize?' Nick asked.

Stone frowned, biting his knuckle. 'Perhaps. That first bullet must have been pretty close, but she might have thought it was just bad marksmanship. But she must know that someone shopped them. What did she say to you?'

'Well, she reckons the whole thing was engineered by Reilly to get rid of her, all right. But her theory is that the best way to convince him that she really is kosher is to go straight back as if nothing had happened.'

'I see her point,' Stone muttered unwillingly. 'No one would put themselves in that kind of jeopardy unless either they were a complete fool, or they were totally innocent and had no reason to suspect any harm.'

'That's what she said,' Nick told him. 'Only she quoted Shakespeare—"whose nature is so far from doing harm that he suspects none".'

Stone smiled briefly. 'She would!'

'She said afterwards that she wished she hadn't,' Nick added. 'It's from *Macbeth*.'

'So?'

'Most actors regard *Macbeth* as unlucky. It's a superstition. Some of them won't even say the name. They refer to it as "the Scottish Play".'

'I don't give a damn about actors' superstitions!' Stone said irritably. 'The point is, what do we do now about Leo?'

'Carry on as before, I suppose,' Nick said. 'She said to tell you that she would stick to the same system of signals.'

'If Reilly doesn't buy her story she won't get a chance to make any signals,' Stone growled bitterly.

There was a silence. Then Nick said quietly,

'Don't think I didn't try to persuade her to give up. But you know Leo . . .'

Stone smiled ruefully. 'Barbed wire and gossamer . . . ?'

'As before,' Nick agreed. 'Well, not quite as before . . .'

Stone drew a deep breath. 'Well, you'd better drop me off somewhere I can get a bus back to Daltry Road.'

Nick nodded and started the engine. 'Tell you what. I'd give a day's pay to see Reilly's face when she walks in.'

CHAPTER SEVEN

As it happened, the first person to see the two women was Patrick Connor—and it took him a few seconds to recognize them. The equipment in the back of Nick's van had included another complete change of clothes and a further selection of wigs; so the two smart city girls strolling down Daltry Road as if on their way home from a Sunday afternoon outing looked very different from the mud-stained creatures whom Nick had picked up—and also from the jeaned and booted hikers the police had seen in the quarry.

Leo had learned from Nick that Reilly and

Liam Connor had got back safely to Birmingham and that the police appeared to have completely lost their trail, but she could not tell Margaret that without arousing her suspicions as to the source of her information; so they had to go through the motions of walking past the house a couple of times, hoping to see some evidence that their friends were still in residence. Reilly's elderly Maxi was nowhere to be seen but, as Leo pointed out, he would have ditched that at the first opportunity.

As they passed the house for the second time Patrick came round the corner of the street. Leo accosted him with,

'Good-evening, Patrick, and how's the family?'

For a few seconds he stared at the two of them as if they were strangers whom he felt he should know but could not place. Then his eyes widened.

'Dear God, it's you two!'

Leo smiled at him. 'Aren't you pleased to see us?'

He glanced up and down the street.

'Are you sure you're not being followed?'

'Quite sure,' Leo told him.

'Did Kevin and Liam make it?' Margaret asked urgently.

'Sure, sure. They got back last night after dark. Kevin has a bullet wound in the arm— one of the swine sneaked round behind him—

131

and Liam had to take him to casualty to get it dressed; but he had the sense to take him to Wrexham so they'll not trace him here.' Once again he glanced around him. 'Come on in the house, will you. We can't stand talking here.'

'I thought you'd never ask!' murmured Leo.

Patrick unlocked the front door and ushered them into the hall. As he closed the door behind them he called,

'Kevin, Liam, come here now and see who I've found on the doorstep!'

The two men came out of the back kitchen. Reilly had his arm in a sling. Liam's face when he recognized them was a mask of blank incomprehension, but the expressions chased themselves across Reilly's like someone flicking through the pages of a picture book. He settled at length on a look of wary congratulation.

'You made it, then.'

'You might look a bit happier about it!' Margaret exclaimed.

'I expect it's a bit of a shock,' Leo said gently. 'After all, you weren't expecting us back, were you?'

Reilly shot her a sideways look. 'I was not. I couldn't see any way you could break out of that place with the police all round you. How did you do it?'

Patrick moved past them to the kitchen door.

'Come on through. You'll be wanting a cup

132

of tea, and something to eat, I expect.'

'Great!' Margaret exclaimed, following him. 'I'm famished!'

So, while Patrick cooked sausages and eggs on the greasy gas cooker, they sat over mugs of tea and Margaret told the story of their escape. When she came to Nick's part in it Reilly grunted.

'That fellow again! I don't like the way he keeps cropping up.'

'At least he does "crop up" when he's needed,' Leo said crisply. 'We'd have had no chance if we'd had to rely on you.'

'That's not fair!' Liam cried. 'Kevin was wounded, I had to get him to hospital. Anyway, if we'd stayed any longer the police would have had all of us.'

'Oh quite,' Leo agreed innocently. 'I just meant that it's lucky I have my own people to call on.'

'And what I'm saying is,' Reilly continued, 'that these people of yours seem to know too much and get away with too much.'

'What are you suggesting by that remark?' Leo asked, her eyes fixed on him.

'I want to know who shopped us to the police. They didn't turn up there by accident.'

'Yes,' Leo said softly. 'That's what I want to know, too.'

In the silence her eyes went round the faces of the three men. Then Liam said,

'You're not trying to say it was one of us?

133

You don't think we'd betray our own people!'

Leo looked at him. 'You don't imagine it was me, do you? I'm wanted for murder, remember. If it ever comes to trial I haven't got a hope in hell. There's nothing ahead of me but twenty years inside if the police catch up with me.'

'Then you are suggesting it was one of us,' Reilly said harshly.

'Just a minute!' Patrick put in. 'If that's what you're thinking, I must be the prime suspect. I'm the only one who wasn't around at the time.'

'Well?' Leo said quietly.

He returned her gaze. 'I can't prove it wasn't me—but you can't prove it was. So where do we go from here?'

Once again there was a silence. They were all aware of having reached a position of stalemate. It was Reilly who spoke eventually.

'You're all forgetting, we weren't the only ones who knew about the job. The orders came from up the line. There must be three or four people in the chain of command who knew. It's there we should be looking for our traitor.'

'But why?' Liam asked. 'Why would they do it?'

Reilly gave him a bitter look. 'You know how many of our people are inside because of the "supergrass" trials—and you know what sort of inducements were offered to those men to betray their comrades. And you ask me why!'

'So,' said Patrick. 'That's where we look. How do we start?'

'We'll talk about that later,' Reilly told him. 'First we have to decide what's going to happen to these two.'

'Happen to us?' Margaret said sharply.

'You must see you can't stay here,' Reilly said. 'There's half the police forces in the country looking for you. You're a liability rather than a help now.'

Margaret looked at Leo. Somewhat to her surprise Leo said quietly,

'What do you suggest?'

Reilly leaned forward, his manner almost cajoling.

'There's a friend of ours coming over from Ireland in a day or two. There will be someone with him who'll have transport. He'll get you back to Ireland and you'll be taken care of there. There's plenty you can be doing, and you'll be safe into the bargain.'

Leo looked from him to the other two.

'Do I have a choice?'

'Sure you do,' Reilly told her. 'You have a choice between us—and the police.'

Leo nodded, smiling faintly. 'Very well. When do we go, and how?'

'There's no need for you to worry about that. When the time comes you'll be taken to the place and told what to do. For the next day or two stay out of sight, that's all.'

They ate the food Patrick had prepared and watched the television news, which showed shots of police still searching holiday cottages in the vicinity of the quarry. Then Leo declared that she was ready for bed and would like a hot bath. Margaret followed her upstairs but, not being much addicted to soap and water, settled for a quick wash and went to their room. Leo ran the bath and undressed, but instead of getting in she leaned over and sloshed her hand around in the water a few times to simulate the right noises. Then she drew her dressing-gown around her, took a tooth-glass and a nail-file from the shelf and knelt down in the corner of the room. A moment or two of careful levering with the file raised one edge of the linoleum and she peeled it back to reveal the floorboards beneath. Then, stretching herself almost flat on the floor she placed the glass on the boards and pressed her ear to it. The bathroom was immediately above the kitchen and she could hear the murmur of the men's voices but to start with there was too much noise from the water pipes for her to make out the words. At length, however, the noise died away and her ear became attuned to the voices. Reilly was saying,

'. . . sooner we get them away the better. We don't want to take any risks after the Horseman gets here.'

'When's he arriving?' Patrick asked.

'His flight gets into Speke at 10.15 on Saturday. They'll drive down to the sale and we'll meet them there. After the business is over the girls can go back in the box . . .'

From the bedroom Margaret called,

'Beth, are you going to be all night in that bath? You know I can't sleep with the light on.'

Leo rose swiftly and gave the bath water a stir.

'I won't be long,' she called back. 'Put the light out if you want. I can go to bed in the dark.'

She replaced the lino carefully. It was old and had cracked where she had turned it back. She hoped that no one would notice. Then she stepped reluctantly into the lukewarm water and washed herself quickly, thinking as she did so how good it would be to relax in a hot tub.

Leo spent most of the following day lying on her bed. Reilly had made it very clear that neither of them was to go outside, but she had persuaded him to buy her a copy of the *Daily Telegraph* and passed most of the time doing the crossword puzzle and occasionally reading some of its more right-wing articles aloud to Margaret, with suitably scathing comments. By afternoon the combination of the, to her, totally incomprehensible clues, and the repeated click-click of Leo's biro as she thumbed the spring which retracted the nib had irritated Margaret so much that she

137

exclaimed,

'For God's sake, will you put the beastly thing away! I don't know why you wanted it in the first place.'

'Because it's the only crossword I can do,' Leo said equably. 'Anyway, I've finished now.'

The rain of the day before had given way to a sultry, overcast sky, with the promise of thunder and the small bedroom had become almost unbearably stuffy. Leo rose and picked up the amber scarf from the dressing-table and began to mop her face and neck with it.

'Let's have some air in here!' she exclaimed and flung open the window.

Margaret sat up abruptly. 'Beth, will you come away from there! You don't know who might be watching.'

Leo laughed at her teasingly. 'There's no one out there but the neighbours, and they're used to the sight of us by now.' She fanned herself with the paper. 'God, it's hot!'

In the window of the house opposite Don Stevens jerked to attention and said,

'There she is!'

Stone swung his legs off the bed and joined him swiftly.

'That's it!' he said exultantly. 'She's got a message for us.'

'What do we do now?' Don asked.

'Wait until dark,' Stone told him. 'Amber scarf—meaning no immediate danger. When they're all asleep I'll go and have a nose round.'

Leo turned back to Margaret with a shrug and moved away from the window.

'Oh, all right, if it's worrying you. Come on, let's go downstairs.'

In the kitchen Leo looked around her with distaste.

'This place is a tip!' she declared. 'Come on. I need something to occupy me.'

With one of her sudden changes of mood she flung herself into tidying up and by the time she had finished not only was the dustbin in the back yard full, but beside it stood a cardboard box full of old newspapers, including the *Telegraph* on which she had expended so much thought.

*   *   *

Stone waited until after midnight, when all the lights in the front of the house opposite had been off for more than an hour. Then he pulled on a dark jersey and pushed his feet into a pair of trainers and slipped quietly out into the street. At the end of each terrace of houses there was a passage which led back to a narrow alley running between the back yards of this street and those of the next. Stone strolled casually to the entrance of the passage nearest to the house where Leo was, paused for a moment and then disappeared into it. In the alley he counted the backs of the houses until he was behind the right one and stood still in the almost total darkness between the high walls. There was no sound from any of the houses around. Not even a dog had barked. After a moment, he reached up and gripped the top of the wall and pulled himself up until he could see over it. The back of the house, like the front, was in darkness. He scrabbled with his toes against the brickwork and hoisted himself onto the top of the wall and then dropped soundlessly to the ground on the far side.

Here, once again, he remained motionless until he was sure that no one was stirring and his eyes, well accustomed now to the faint light of reflected street lamps from the overcast sky, had made out the shapes of what had once been a tool-shed, a dilapidated bike and a path leading to the back door of the house. He picked his way silently towards it but almost fell over the black dustbin in the shadows. He crouched against the wall, clutching the lid, and thanked God for plastic bins. When his pulse had steadied again he felt carefully around the bin and smiled to himself as he found the cardboard box. Only then did he risk using the tiny penlight torch which he had brought with him, just long enough to identify Leo's handwriting on the crossword page of the paper he wanted. With the paper tucked safely into the waistband of his trousers he retraced his steps, swung himself over the wall in one smooth movement and dropped into the alley. Within ten minutes of leaving he was back again in his own room.

It took him, with Don's help, a good deal longer than that to piece together the message which Leo had traced out by making a tiny pinhole under certain words or letters in the paper. The biro was a special Triple S issue which had been placed in the pocket of the jeans provided for her when she 'escaped' from Risley; and the clicking which had so irritated Margaret had been the operation of the mechanism which flicked out a tiny needle.

When it was finally complete Stone looked at it with some disappointment. He had hoped that it would signal the end of his long vigil and Leo's readiness to relinquish the role she was playing. It seemed to promise neither. He read it aloud to Don.

'Expect arrival code-name The Horseman, Speke, Saturday, 15th, 10.15 hrs.'

*   *   *

Bright and early on Saturday morning Nick, accompanied by Viv Vivian, found himself once again heading up the M6. On arrival at Speke he left Viv in the car to keep an eye on people arriving and departing and presented himself at the main information desk. For once, he was able to use his official ID which rapidly got him through to air traffic control where he learned that the only flight due in at 10.15 was a cargo ferry from Dublin. A brief study of the cargo manifest gave him the clue he was looking for. One of the items was a horse, being brought over by an Irish breeder for sale in England.

A few words with a friendly official procured him the use of an empty room in a building which overlooked the cargo bay where the aircraft would be unloaded. The flight came in on time and Nick hunched himself against the window, a pair of field-glasses in his hand and a small camera ready on the sill beside him, as the loading ramp was lowered. It was not long before the horse-box rolled slowly down the ramp. Nick swore to himself as he struggled to make out the faces of the two men in the front of it, but for once he was in luck. The movement had apparently upset the animal inside, because the box stopped and one man got down and went round to the rear and let down the tail-board. Nick let out a sharp exclamation of triumph as he saw him and grabbed for the camera. By the time the horse had been pacified and the tail-board secured again he had as many pictures as he needed of both men.

Leaving them to complete the necessary formalities he hurried back to the car and handed the camera to Viv.

'I need to get these processed for identification and passed to Pascoe as soon as possible. I can't put a name to it, but one of the faces is very familiar. You can get a flight from here back to either Heathrow or Gatwick—and while you're waiting for it, get all the information you can about the owner of the horse that came in on the 10.15 cargo ferry from Dublin. How often does he ship horses over, where do they go, who comes with them—anything that might be useful. I'll keep track of our friends and report back.'

When Viv had gone Nick called Triple S HQ on the scrambler and told them what he had seen. He had just finished when the horse-box drove slowly out of the airport gates and headed for the M62.

*　　　*　　　*

After Leo's return to Daltry Road, Stone decided he ought to have his own car. He had an uneasy feeling that when something happened it could be with very little warning and having his own transport gave him a slightly greater sense of security. He collected the car on the day after Leo had left her message. It was a Ford Escort, several years old, which, to the casual observer, had seen better days. If anyone seeing it parked outside Stone's lodgings had happened to look under the bonnet or in the boot they would have been astonished to discover a high-performance engine, tuned to maximum efficiency, and a package of electronic gadgetry including a radio scrambler phone and tracking equipment.

By a coincidence, Liam Connor came home that day with a new car too. At least, it was new to him, but, like Stone's Escort, Liam's Cortina was well past its prime.

As Saturday approached Stone's sense of uneasiness increased. He knew that Nick was covering the Speke end, but felt sure that there would be some move from Reilly and Co. as well; and he was not reassured by the fact that he had not caught a glimpse of Leo since she had signalled him about the message. His extra vigilance was rewarded when, early on the Saturday morning, the front door of the house opposite suddenly opened and Leo appeared with Margaret, Reilly and Liam. Patrick Connor, Stone had observed, had left the previous day and not returned.

Resisting the temptation to run downstairs and get into his own car Stone called Max and Don, still patiently on watch in the old factory where they had set up their headquarters, and waited until the Cortina turned the corner. Only then did he hurry down to the car and switch on the tracking receiver. Following the bleep from Leo's replacement bug he nosed through the Saturday rush-hour traffic until he found himself out on the open road to the west of the city. A change in the pitch of the bleep warned him that his target had stopped and a moment later he saw the Cortina ahead of him, drawn up in a lay-by behind a Range Rover which was towing a trailer horse-box. As he cruised past he saw that Patrick Connor was at the wheel of the second vehicle and that Leo and Margaret were just being ushered into the back seat by Reilly. In his rear-view mirror, a moment later, he saw Liam ease the Cortina out into the flow of traffic. He reached for his microphone and called Max, knowing that he was somewhere nearby.

'Theta One, this is Delta One. Targets have separated, Cortina now heading south with driver only. Please follow.'

'Roger, Delta One,' came the reply. Then, a few seconds later 'Target in sight. I am following.'

Stone pulled into a side-road and waited until he saw the Range Rover go by. He gave it time to get well ahead and set off once again in pursuit. The track led him northwards and onto the M6, but then its course became erratic, leaving the motorway at the next junction and performing a wide loop to rejoin it further on. Stone's jaw tightened. There was only one explanation—Reilly suspected that he might be followed and was checking up.

Eventually they left the motorway again and Stone had to close the distance in order to follow the signal through the Cheshire countryside. After some time he passed a ruined castle on a low hill and signpost pointing to Beeston; then the signal note changed again and he guessed that they had come to their destination. He rounded a bend and came upon a collection of buildings surrounded by concrete pens holding cattle and pigs, clearly a country market. Stone raised his eyebrows and muttered—'Hell of a long way to come to buy a pig!' He pulled into the car-park and looked about him, but the whole area was sprinkled with trailers, many of them pulled by Range Rovers, and he could not see which was the one he had been following. The bleep was on the move again, and he guessed Leo was on foot and, presumably, heading into the market.

He left the car, pocketing the portable direction-finder, and headed in the same direction. The market was crowded and he could not use the gadget without attracting attention, so for a while he searched up and down the pathways between the pens in the hope of spotting Leo or one of her companions, only checking the signal occasionally. In a long building horses stood in stalls while prospective buyers strolled between them, but there was no sign of her there, either. Finally, he found a secluded corner behind one of the cattle pens and pulled out the direction-finder again. To his dismay, he found that the regular bleep had ceased. He swore softly and moved to a fresh position, hoping that the signal might have been shielded in some way, but the thing was still dead. He glanced at his watch. There had hardly been time for Leo to return to the car, or to some other vehicle, and get out of range; so there were only two possible explanations. Either his direction-finder was faulty, or for some reason which he did not wish to contemplate Leo's bug had once again ceased to transmit.

He ran back to the car, praying that the first solution was the correct one, and switched on the machine attached to the dashboard. It too was silent.

*   *   *

When they arrived at the market Leo looked about her with interest. In spite of her sophistication, she had had a country girl's upbringing and had never lost her love for that kind of life. As she walked between Reilly and Connor towards the main sale-ring she watched the horses being led from their boxes with a knowledgeable eye. It had been at just such a sale, two years ago, that she had bought Serendipity, the chestnut gelding which she kept at livery near the tiny Surrey cottage to which she retreated whenever she got the chance. She thought wistfully how long it had been since she last rode him, and the thought reminded her that if she wanted ever to ride him again she had better keep her wits about her.

She was sure that it was from here that Reilly intended to ship Margaret and herself off to Ireland and, all through the journey, she had been weighing the implications. After her experience in the quarry she had few doubts about the fate Reilly had in mind for her ultimately and, once across the Irish sea, she did not give much for her chances of avoiding it. On the other hand, she was aware that by going along with Reilly's plan she might uncover some very useful information about how the IRA smuggled their people in and out of the country. Her sense of self-preservation told her that the knowledge would be of little use if she never got the opportunity to pass it on; but at that point her stubborn pride rose up and accused her of cowardice. Finally she had compromised on the plan that she would go on until the last possible moment and trust to luck that she would be able to make a break before it was too late. The question was, how would she recognize that last possible chance?

Margaret, who had been fidgeting all through the last half-hour of the journey, had made a bee-line for the ladies' room as soon as they arrived. Now Leo saw her pushing her way through the crowd towards them, her small face puckered into an expression of furious determination; but it wasn't until their eyes met that Leo realized that Margaret's change of mood had something to do with her.

'Kevin, I must talk to you—it's urgent!' Margaret exclaimed, tugging at his arm.

He glanced from her to Leo and then allowed her to draw him away out of earshot. Leo watched them, feeling the hair rise on the back of her neck.

'Why, hallo there, Patrick! It's good to see you again!'

A tall, reddish-haired man was edging his way towards them through the crowd.

'Michael!' Connor responded. 'Well, where have you sprung from?'

The two men shook hands with a contrived effusiveness which offended Leo's professional sensibilities. 'Oh great!' she muttered inwardly. 'Don't call us, we'll call you!'

The moment of inattention lost her the initiative. As the thoughts crossed her mind she felt the cold muzzle of Reilly's pistol pressed into her back.

'Don't move, and don't call out,' he said softly in her ear. 'Maybe I wouldn't get far if I had to use this but at least I'd make sure you didn't have a chance to tell anyone what you know.'

The red-headed man swung towards her.

'Who is she?' he demanded.

'That's what we're just about to find out!' Reilly told him.

Leo moved a fraction of a pace forward, easing the pressure of the gun against her ribs.

'What the hell has got into you now?' she

149

inquired coldly.

'Oh no!' Reilly said, shaking his head. 'From now on I'm asking the questions.' He looked at the man called Michael. 'Where's the Horseman?'

'Took the grey to the stables.'

Reilly glanced at Connor. 'Find him. Tell him we may have been followed. He's to make his own way and meet up with us at the next rendezvous. Then take her,' he jerked his head towards Margaret, 'to the car and keep her there till we come.'

'What are you going to do?' Margaret asked, white-faced.

'What I should have done days ago,' Reilly returned. He looked again at Michael. 'Where's your box?'

'In the car-park—over there.' The big man nodded in the general direction.

'Right, we'll take her there. Come on.'

The red-headed man took Leo's arm with something which might, at a distance, have been taken for protective chivalry and led her towards the car-park. Reilly followed a pace behind, the gun in his hand concealed under a folded raincoat. When they reached the horse-box Michael opened the door in the side and shoved Leo through. The interior of the box smelt of straw and fresh dung, smells which in other circumstances Leo would have found pleasantly familiar. At the end was a locker which formed a kind of bench. The big man pushed her onto it and Reilly came and stood looking down at her.

Leo leaned back against the partition behind her and met his gaze.

'Come on, then. What's it all about? Or are you just showing off for the benefit of your new friend?'

'You tell us,' Reilly replied grimly. 'Starting with how your man Marriot comes to be lurking about out there somewhere.'

'Marriot!' Leo exclaimed. Her mind raced as she tried to follow the implications. She had assumed until that moment that Stone was the one who had been seen and, somehow, recognized.

'Margaret walked straight into him not five minutes ago,' Reilly said. 'Now, you told us that no one, not even Marriot, knew where you were staying.'

'I told no one,' Leo said firmly. 'The fool must have followed us.'

'You said you were sure you weren't being followed when you came back that night.'

'So?' Leo shrugged. 'I was thinking of the police. Marriot's good at his job. So what? He's safe enough. He won't betray you.'

'Then what's he doing here, spying on us?' Reilly demanded.

'Look, he thinks he's in love with me. He's probably doing some big, macho protective thing. Why don't you go out there and find him? Let me talk to him.'

Reilly shook his head. 'No, it won't do. He didn't follow you from Birmingham, because I made damn sure no one was following us. If he'd been anywhere in sight I'd have spotted him. And you didn't tell him where to go because you didn't know yourself. Unless . . .' He turned to the red-haired man. 'Search her.'

Leo submitted without resistance as he pulled her to her feet and ran clumsy hands over her body, knowing that any show of fight would only make the process more unpleasant in the end. The stubby fingers probed her jeans pockets and pulled open the front of her shirt.

'Nothing obvious,' Michael said finally.

'OK.' Reilly looked at her with narrowed eyes. 'You'd best tell us where it is. Or have you ever been strip-searched? Oh, it's something you get used to in prison! Only here we've no female wardress to carry it out—and no nice, hygienic polythene gloves to put on when we get to the delicate bits . . .'

He paused, staring at her. A sick revulsion crept through her stomach, but logic told her that it was possible they might do all that and still find nothing. In which case . . .

She lifted her head and looked at him with eyes brilliant with contempt.

'So that's it, is it, Reilly? Of course, I should have known all along.' She began to unbutton the front of her shirt. 'Come on, then. Amuse yourself!'

Reilly was breathing hard and she saw him pass his tongue over his lips. Lust—or fear? She held his gaze with deliberate provocation.

'The hair!' he said suddenly. 'Try the hair. It comes off, you know.'

'Does it so?'

The big man grabbed at the auburn wig and, as he yanked it loose, a small metal object the size of a button clattered onto the floor of the horse-box; falling, as luck would have it, onto an area clear of straw. Reilly pounced on it and picked it up.

'So there we are!' he exclaimed triumphantly. 'I knew you were a phoney all along.' He dropped the bug back onto the floor and smashed it under his heel. Then, for a long moment, he gazed at her in silence. When he spoke again the exultation had left his voice, leaving it deadly cold. 'Now, let's start from the beginning. Who are you, and who are you working for?'

'Look,' Leo said, angrily, 'Marriot planted that on me. I didn't even know it was there.'

Reilly caught her across the face with a back-handed slap that cracked her head back against the partition.

'Now I know you're lying. Come on, I'm not playing around any longer.'

He hit her again, twice, repeating, 'Who are you? Who sent you?'

She looked up at him, licking a trickle of blood from the corner of her mouth.

153

'Do you really think you're going to make me talk—here?'

'She's right,' the other man put in. 'These things take time—and they make a noise. Leave her to me. When I get her home we'll have all the time we need . . .' He drew Reilly away to the far end of the van and spoke too softly for her to hear.

'How do you think you're going to get her through customs?' Reilly demanded. 'You may have her out of sight, but you won't be able to keep her quiet.'

'Oh, won't I?' the red-haired man said. 'Don't worry. We're prepared for this sort of thing.'

He opened a small cupboard built into the partition and took out a box. Inside was a hypodermic syringe and an ampule.

'It's supposed to be for sedating the horses if they get restive,' he said, grinning. 'A shot of this and she'll be out till we're back in Dublin.'

Leo watched him filling the syringe and knew that once he succeeded in injecting her her last chance would be gone. She glanced at Reilly. He, too, was watching Michael. She sensed that he was reluctant to let her go and while his mind was occupied with that thought the hand holding the gun had relaxed. It was a faint hope, but she snatched at it. In a single movement she thrust herself forward and kicked out as high and as hard as she could, using the strength and suppleness of her

154

dancer's body and the training provided by the experts at Triple S to deliver a blow as powerful and accurate as a machine. The gun flew out of Reilly's hand and as his body slewed away from her she hit him in the kidneys with a double-handed rabbit punch that felled him to his knees.

By that time, however, the other man was moving in on her, the syringe in his right hand, the left reaching out to grab hold of her. She seized his wrist and jerked him towards her, hoping to use his own momentum to unbalance him; but she might as well have tried to unbalance Nelson's Column. He broke her grip with a single downwards jab and the next second his hand was around her throat, forcing her back against the side of the van and stifling her cries for help. She tried to kick out again, but the length of his arm was such that she could not reach him with her knee while he was too close for her to employ the full length of her leg. The he threw his whole weight against her and she was pinioned against the wall, helpless and rapidly losing consciousness.

*   *   *

Stone was still staring in impotent fury at the direction-finder when his radio crackled into life.

'Delta One, this is Delta Two,' said Nick's

155

voice. 'Do you read me? Come in, please.'

Stone grabbed the microphone. 'Delta One here. Where are you, Delta Two?'

'Thank God!' he heard Nick say. Then, 'Delta One, this is Delta Two. I guess I must be at the same place as you. Beeston Market?'

'How the hell . . . ?' Stone exclaimed.

'Listen!' Nick, said urgently. 'I think Omega may be in danger. I picked up the target at Speke, according to your message, and followed him here. There are two men, and one of them looks very familiar. I can't give him a name, but I'm sure he was one of the faces that were circulated a few months back as possible INLA men working in the UK. Small, very slight, fair . . .'

'Slattery,' said Stone, whose memory for faces and names was on of his greatest assets.

'Right!' returned Nick. 'Anyway, he's here. They came over with a big white horse, supposedly for sale. I followed them from the car-park and walked slap into the Donelly girl. She recognized me, of course, and smelt a rat at once. I tried to stop her, but she ran like a rabbit and I lost her in the crowd. If she's got back to Reilly and told him it'll give him all the excuse he needs to get rid of Omega. Is she with them?'

'Yes, and now I'll tell you the really bad news,' Stone said grimly. 'Omega's bleep went off the air a couple of minutes ago.'

'Oh Christ!' Nick muttered miserably. 'Why

the hell didn't you call me and let me know you were in the area?'

'Come to that, why didn't you call me?' Stone returned. 'But never mind that now. Where are you parked?'

'North side of the parking area.'

'What about the vehicle Slattery and his mate arrived in?'

'About two rows ahead of me. It's a horse-box with an Irish registration.'

'Right,' Stone said. 'You get after Slattery and keep tabs on him. I'll search for Leo.'

'No. We'd better both concentrate on Leo,' Nick replied.

'Do as I say!' Stone's tone was crisp. 'We can't risk losing Slattery. Besides, they know you but they don't know me.'

There was a fractional pause, then Nick said. 'OK. Delta Two out.' Partners and friends they might be, but at times like this there was never any argument about who was the senior.

Stone got out of the car and headed for the north side of the parking area. Failing any better clues, it seemed as good a place to start looking as any other.

He found the horse-box with its red Irish registration plates quite quickly and strolled casually along the length of it. From inside he heard a scuffle and a muffled thud. It could have been a restless horse—but had not Nick said he had seen them leading the horse away?

Stone moved to the personal door at the side and paused, listening. The thuds were repeated. He opened the door silently and stepped inside. Towards the back of the box Reilly was leaning against the side, coughing painfully. Immediately in front of Stone Leo was almost hidden by the large form of a red-haired Irishman.

'Look out!' Reilly gasped, and the other man swung round.

'What do you want?' he demanded.

Stone smiled deprecatingly. 'Heard noises,' he explained, in the 'officers' mess' voice he had once spent so much effort and anguish in acquiring. 'Thought you might be having some trouble.'

The Irishman came towards him. 'No trouble,' he said and grinned. 'Just a bit of horse-play.' He laughed loudly. 'Horse-play! Get it?'

Behind him Stone could see Leo slumped against the partition, her eyes half closed. The Irishman's laugh ceased abruptly as Stone's fist caught him in the stomach and as he doubled over he finished the job with a karate chop that dropped him like a bullock in an abattoir. The hypodermic syringe flew out of his hand and smashed. Stone jumped over his body and turned to deal with Reilly but as he did so the tail-board of the lorry went down with a rattling crash and Reilly scuttled down it and ran off across the car-park. Stone ran to the

158

back of the box but as he reached it Reilly turned and he saw that he had picked up the gun, which he now levelled in Stone's direction. Stone ducked back, and when he looked again the Irishman was already among the people making their way into the sale-ring. Stone had no doubt that to pursue him there would result in a shoot-out, with the inevitable loss of innocent lives. He turned back into the box to look at Leo.

She had sunk down onto the bench, breathing fast and shallow through open lips. He ran back to her and knelt by her side. Her sleeve was ripped and through the tear he could see the small globule of blood where the needle had punctured the skin.

'Leo!' he said urgently. 'What was it?'

She swallowed and forced a smile. 'It's OK. Just a sedative—and he didn't get much into me. I'll be all right.'

He pulled her to her feet.

'Come on. Let's get you out of here before Reilly gets hold of the rest of them.'

He half carried her down the ramp but as they crossed the car-park the strength seemed to come back to her legs.

'It's OK,' she said, as he helped into the front seat of the Escort. 'I'm fine. He half choked me, that was the main trouble.'

As he started the engine she sat up suddenly.

'Look!'

Following her pointing finger he saw the Range Rover, now without the trailer, heading towards the gate and, in the brief glimpse he had of the occupants, recognized Reilly.

'That's them!' he said.

He let in the clutch and felt the wheels spin as the powerful engine took hold. After the recent rain the ground was soft and he had to nurse the Escort over the muddy track that led to the entrance. The Range Rover, built for such conditions, had gained a good lead by the time they reached the road, but once on firm ground Stone set about closing the gap. He glanced at Leo. Her eyes were wide open and her lips, though cut and swollen from Reilly's blows, were set firm.

'You'll find a gun in the glove box,' he told her.

She nodded and reached for it. Out of the corner of his eye he watched her check that it was fully loaded and marvelled at the steadiness of her hands. They were on a stretch of open road now, running straight and flat alongside a canal but separated from it by a grassy bank. There were no other cars in sight.

'We'll take them here!' he said, and Leo nodded.

Stone accelerated and moved out to overtake the Range Rover, but as he drew almost level the back door of the other vehicle was flung open and he saw Connor crouched inside with a rifle at his shoulder.

'Get down!' he screamed at Leo, but as he spoke a bullet shattered the windscreen and thudded into the back seat between them and, almost simultaneously, another hit his off-side front tyre. Temporarily blinded by the crazed glass of the windscreen he felt the car slew violently across the road, mount the bank and then become, for an instant, airborne. A split second later it landed with a shuddering splash in the middle of the canal.

As the water began to rise around their waists they both fought to free themselves from their seat-belts but, when the car came to rest with a slight jolt on the bed of the canal, they found to their relief that the top foot of the interior was still above water. He saw Leo take a deep breath and duck beneath the surface and a second later her hip thrust briefly against him as she wriggled out through the window. As soon as he was sure that she was free he followed her example.

By the time he had floundered through the muddy water to the bank she had already hauled herself out. As she stood looking down at him, her lips twisted into a lop-sided grin.

'You know, Stone, we're going to have to stop meeting like this. I don't know what it is, but every time I run into you these days, you end up throwing yourself in the river.'

Within minutes they were surrounded by a small crowd of passing motorists, anglers and the crews of two cabin cruisers whose further progress along the canal was blocked by the submerged Escort; but it was almost an hour before they had finished explaining, first of all to them and later to the police, that they had had a blow-out and lost control. By that time it was obviously hopeless to try and pick up Reilly's trail and, with the radio and the scrambler phone at the bottom of the canal, there was no way of contacting Nick or Pascoe. They accepted the offer of a lift into Nantwich, arranged to have the car dragged out of the canal, and checked into the Lamb Hotel.

The receptionist regarded them with understandable doubt as they approached, still damp and bedraggled from their ducking, but her attitude changed when Stone explained their circumstances. Fortunately, the story of the accident also accounted for Leo's torn clothes and bruised face. She had remained clear-headed and composed throughout but Stone could see that she was exhausted. Without thinking twice about it he booked her in as Mrs Stone and they went up to their room. As soon as the door closed behind them he took her in his arms and held her tenderly.

'Listen,' he murmured after a moment. 'We've both got to have a change of clothes. You stay here and rest. I'll go out and buy something for both of us.'

She looked up at him, amused.

'Do you think you can cope with choosing a

female wardrobe?'

He grinned. 'I can't go far wrong with a pair of jeans and a T-shirt, can I? And the usual under-pinnings, of course. What size?'

'Thirty-six—twenty-four—thirty-six,' she told him, 'and size five feet.'

'Right.' He released her and turned to the door. 'Thank God for plastic credit cards!' Then he stopped and turned back. 'Don't open the door to anyone except me.'

'I won't,' she promised. 'I'm going to have a shower.'

He found a shop nearby which could supply everything he needed for them both and within twenty minutes he was back. She opened the door to him wrapped, sarong-style, in a bath towel; flushed and damp and smelling sweetly of soap. He kissed her, but she wrinkled her nose at him.

'I'm sorry, sweetheart, but you still have a distinct odour of the Shropshire Union.'

He laughed. 'My turn for a shower.'

When he came out of the bathroom she was lying under the sheet on one of the twin beds. He thought for a moment that she was asleep and began quietly unpacking the clothes he had bought. After a few seconds he realized that she had opened her eyes and was watching him. He grinned at her.

'You know, if this case goes on much longer I'm going to end up with webbed feet.'

She shook her head gently. 'Water on the

brain.'

'Or both, even,' he agreed.

'Of course, that being so,' she murmured, 'You've got all the wrong gear there. That isn't what you need at all.'

'Oh?' he asked, unwisely. 'What do I need?'

She smiled sweetly. 'Drain-pipe trousers and a pair of pumps, stupid.'

He picked up a shoe and made to throw it at her, then changed his mind and went round the bed and took her in his arms. Her skin was warm and velvet soft but as she moved to hold him he felt the smooth glide of the muscles underneath it. It was like embracing a sleepy tigress. He rubbed his face in her hair and murmured,

'Oh Leo, they knew what they were doing when they christened you!'

At the back of his mind was the thought that he ought to contact Pascoe; but he decided that it could wait till later—much later.

CHAPTER EIGHT

It was after two by the time Stone got through to Pascoe. Leo was sitting up in bed finishing off a late lunch of turkey sandwiches and a bottle of chilled Pouilly-Fuissé and he saw her cock an ear and grin as Pascoe came on the line. Even from that distance she could hear the cutting edge on Pascoe's normally urbane tone.

'What the hell have you been up to?' Pascoe demanded. 'Delta Two called in nearly two hours ago and said he couldn't raise you and that you'd lost touch with Omega.'

'Yes, well, there's no need to worry on that score, sir,' Stone told him. 'I've—made contact with Omega.'

He heard a sound like a small sneeze, as Leo choked a giggle in her wineglass.

'Why haven't you been in touch before this?' Pascoe wanted to know. 'What's been going on? And why are you calling on an open line?'

'I'm sorry about that, sir,' Stone replied. 'I'm afraid my scrambler's at the bottom of the Shropshire Union Canal at the moment.'

'And where are you?'

'Nantwich, sir.'

'And Omega?'

'She's here, with me.'

'Is she all right?'

'Yes, she's fine, sir—well, give or take the odd black eye. But I'm afraid we've lost our other friends.'

There was a short but eloquent silence at the other end of the line.

'That makes two of you!' Pascoe said eventually. 'Right. Get Omega to Crewe and put her on the first train to London. I'll send Waller to meet her at King's Cross. She can fill me in with what's been going on at your end. You'll find Delta Two at Hereford police station. Join him there and he'll put you in the picture. Report back to me when you get there. Understood?'

'Understood, sir,' Stone said, and put the phone down. He looked regretfully at Leo.

'You're going home. Pascoe wants you.'

*   *   *

Three hours later Stone found Nick sitting behind a desk in an office in Hereford police station.

'That's a relief,' he commented. 'When Pascoe said Hereford nick I thought they might have you shut up in the cells again.'

'Not this time,' Nick replied. 'But I gather from the same source you've been up to your old tricks again. Look, I know you're fond of the girl, but there's no need to go overboard every time you meet her.'

Stone bared his teeth. 'If anyone else makes a crack about me and water I shall personally stick one on him!'

The door opened and a man in inspector's uniform put his head in.

'Ah', he said, 'thought I heard voices. You must be the bloke who tried to navigate the Shropshire Union in a motor-car. Can't stop, got a bit of a panic on.'

As he moved away down the corridor they

could hear him whistling 'Oh be kind to your web-footed friends . . .'

Stone lowered himself into a chair opposite Nick.

'Leo sends her love,' he said, with deliberation.

'How is she?' Nick asked. 'Much the same?'

'Oh, well . . .' Stone let the word hang in the air for a moment. 'Rather less of the barbed wire . . .'

There was a small pause. Then Nick said, 'I see.'

Stone looked away and suddenly wished he had kept his mouth shut.

'Where is she now?' Nick asked.

'Gone back to London. Pascoe wants her for debriefing.'

'Filthy old goat!' Nick muttered, and they both laughed and the moment of tension passed.

'Anyway,' Nick resumed, 'what exactly happened?'

Stone told him. 'How about you?' he asked.

Nick grimaced. 'Much the same story, I'm afraid. I searched high and low for Slattery, but I suppose Donelly or one of the others had warned him off by then. I couldn't see hide nor hair of him. In the end I went back to the car park to try and call you, and just as I got there I saw a squad car drive in. I hung around a bit and found out that someone had had his Jag pinched about twenty minutes earlier. Well, it was a bit of a forlorn hope but it struck me that if I'd been in Slattery's position, expecting to meet up with someone who was going to provide me with transport and then finding that the arrangements had fouled up and I was on my own, my instinct would be to nick the first set of wheels that came to hand. I tried to get hold of you and when I couldn't I called Pascoe, told him what was going on and got his permission to talk to the uniformed boys. When I told them who I thought might have pinched the motor they put out a general alert. I went back to the local nick and waited and about an hour later a call came in to say the Jag had been found abandoned about ten miles away. Then soon after that another report came in. A woman out picnicking with her kids at a local beauty spot not far from where they found the Jag had been held up at gunpoint by a man answering Slattery's description and forced to hand over the keys of her car—a Peugeot estate, this time. It took her a long time to walk to the main road and flag down another car, so by the time we heard about it Slattery was well away. The only clue we've got is that he appears to be heading south, but that could be a bluff, of course. Regional Crime Squad have taken over the whole thing and alerted all neighbouring forces. That's why I moved down here to the HQ. They've set up road-blocks, but with all the country lanes the chances of picking him up are pretty minimal, I'm afraid.'

Stone sighed. 'You know, my son, I get the feeling that between us we've blown this one. Any word from Theta One?'

'Yes, I called him,' Nick said. 'Apparently Liam Connor drove straight back to the house in Daltry Road and went inside. An hour later he left again, on foot, went into the centre of Birmingham and . . .'

Stone put his head in his hands. 'Don't tell me!'

' 'Fraid so. Went into a newsagent's shop, Don waited for him to come out—he never reappeared. Must've gone out by a back entrance. And no one else has been near the Daltry Road house all day.'

'God, what a bloody mess!' Stone muttered. 'We've lost the lot of them.'

A sergeant looked in. ' 'Scuse me, sir, we've got something.'

Nick and Stone rose simultaneously and headed for the main operations room. The inspector was waiting for them.

'We've had a report from one of our mobile units. They've spotted the Peugeot heading south on the B4214 near Bishops Frome. I've told them to keep well out of sight and ordered three plain-clothes patrols to converge on the section of road between Five Bridges and Ledbury. With any luck we should catch them in a pincer movement.'

'Show me where,' Stone demanded.

The inspector pointed to a map spread out on the table in the centre of the room. Stone studied it for a moment and then straightened up.

'Right. We'll take over here. This man is armed and dangerous. Please instruct your men not to approach him.'

The inspector opened his mouth and then shut it again. Stone met his eyes.

'I'm sure you realize that, as officers of Triple S, we do have that prerogative'—he paused fractionally—'even if we do have webbed feet.' He turned to Nick. 'Where's your car?'

Nick was already on his way to the door.

Stone was not keen on being driven by anybody, particularly not at speed, but Nick was one of the few people he was prepared to trust—more or less; which was fortunate considering the pace at which the younger man hurled the Capri along the Herefordshire lanes. As they drove Stone kept in touch with the police cars through the control room at the station. At length one of them reported that he had the Peugeot in sight, still heading south at about forty m.p.h. The other two cars were approaching the same road, but further ahead and closing at a tangent.

'Shall we block the road?' the driver of one asked.

'Not yet,' Stone replied. 'I don't want him alarmed until we're on the spot. Just keep ahead of him and stay in touch.'

'How far?' Nick asked briefly.

Stone studied the map on his knee and did some rapid calculations. Like the other cars, they were approaching the route of the Peugeot at an angle.

'We should join the B4214 in about two minutes,' he replied, '—if you don't put us in the ditch first. By then I reckon he will be about a mile ahead of us.'

The first car came back on the air.

'I think he may have spotted me. He's accelerating. Doing about sixty now.'

'Drop back,' Stone instructed. 'We're within two miles of you. We'll take over.'

The Capri swung onto the B road and as it did so the radio crackled again.

'Hey-up! He's disappeared!'

'What do you mean—disappeared?' Stone demanded.

'We've just come to a long straight stretch. There's no sign of him.'

'Stay there!' Stone ordered sharply.

The tyres howled as they took a long left-hand bend.

'There!' Nick said.

Ahead of them the road ran straight for well over half a mile. About three hundred yards ahead a red Cortina was parked beside a small clump of trees. Nick drew up behind it. Two men were standing among the trees, gazing down a stony track. Stone and Nick left the car and joined them.

'Stone and Marriot, Triple S,' Stone said briefly.

One of the policemen pointed into the trees.

'There it is.'

The track led to the edge of what had once been a gravel pit, now partially reclaimed by gorse and bracken and silver birches. The Peugeot was at the bottom of it, its nose pressed up against the trunk of a young oak, a trickle of steam wavering upwards from under the bent bonnet. It was empty.

'Any sign of the driver?' Stone asked.

'Not since we got here,' the other man replied.

They scrambled down to the car and looked inside. There was no sign of blood; in fact the interior seemed relatively undamaged. The ground round about it, though soft from the recent rain, showed no footprints.

'Bailed out before it went over the edge, at a guess,' Nick commented.

They climbed back to the track. It ran on round the edge of the pit and disappeared into an area of open country.

'Where does that go?' Stone asked the two local men.

'Nowhere in particular,' one of them told him. 'It splits up into various public footpaths. He could have gone four or five ways.'

'Get on your radio and call the control

room,' Stone told him. 'Tell them to send out some dogs and get mobile patrols to block off all the lanes in this area. He can't get far on foot.' He turned to Nick. 'Let's take a look.'

They set off at a steady jog along the track, but the ground here was too well drained to show footprints and before long they found themselves at the point where three different paths diverged. Between them the bracken grew waist-high. Nick looked around.

'He could be hiding up anywhere.'

'Yeah, we're wasting our time,' Stone agreed. 'We may as well wait for the dogs.'

The dogs, when they arrived, picked up the trail without difficulty, but after a mile or so they came to a low-lying pathway where the wet soil had been churned into mud by the passage of horses. Even to the humans the smell of horse hung rank in the air. The dogs cast up and down for a while, but at length their handler had to admit defeat. The long summer day was almost over and under the trees it was already dusk; and Stone's stomach was reminding him that he had had very little to eat that day except some turkey sandwiches. They decided to call off the search until morning and rely on patrolling the lanes around the area.

Stone and Nick spent the night back at the station, taking turns to sleep on a camp-bed in an empty office; but they were both awake when a call came through a little before seven from a village about four miles from where they had found the Peugeot.

'Just had a report from one of the local milkmen,' the sergeant told them over the phone. 'Apparently he went to deliver milk to an isolated bungalow about two miles away. When he got there, he saw that a light in one of the rooms was being switched on and off, making an SOS signal. He managed to gain entry and found the elderly couple who own the place tied up to chairs in the living-room. The old chap had managed to work his chair across the room to an electric point where a lamp was plugged in, and he was switching it on and off with his toe. According to the story he got from the old people, a man answering the description of the bloke we're looking for turned up on their doorstep late yesterday evening and said his car had broken down and could he use their phone. When they let him in he pulled a gun on them. He forced the lady of the house to cook him a meal, then tied them up and calmly went to sleep in their bedroom. They were too terrified to try anything while he was there, in case he woke up. About 5 a.m. he got up, helped himself to breakfast, took the keys of their car and shoved off.'

'What kind of car?' Stone asked.

'VW Polo, registration number PYG 665V.'

'And where has this little pyggy gone, I wonder,' muttered Nick.

A visit to the hospital where the two old people had been taken to recover confirmed beyond doubt that their visitor had been Slattery; but in spite of an ever-widening net of police check points it was two days before the VW was discovered in the station car-park at Cheltenham. Stone and Marriot met Pascoe at a hotel near the town for a conference.

Once they were seated Pascoe placed his elbows on the arms of his chair and laced his fingers together in his familiar pose.

'Well, gentlemen, what next?'

Nick shook his head. 'God knows, sir. He could be anywhere by now.'

'On the other hand,' Stone said thoughtfully, 'he could still be somewhere quite close.'

Pascoe looked at him. 'Why do you say that?'

'Well, doesn't the station car-park strike you as a bit obvious?' Stone inquired. 'Maybe he just wanted us to think he'd got on a train.'

'I agree with you,' Pascoe nodded, 'and it happens to fit with another bit of information I have. I spoke to Leonora this morning and she remembers Reilly telling Connor that he wanted him to go to Gloucestershire. She says that from the way he spoke she got the impression that Connor already knew why.'

The two men opposite him simultaneously

175

straightened in their chairs and cast off their look of despondency.

'So the trail's not cold yet,' Nick said.

'Not quite,' Pascoe agreed. 'The next question, of course, is what are Reilly and Slattery and Co. after in Gloucestershire?'

The answer came from both men in unison. 'GCHQ?'

'It seems an obvious possibility, although it's hard to see quite what they aim to achieve. They are, after all, terrorists, not spies. However, I have already warned GCHQ to take extra security precautions; and the same warning has gone out to all other military or governmental installations in the area. Our job is still to find Slattery and the others before they get a chance to put their plan, whatever it is, into effect. I've already spoken to local police chiefs and they are going to institute an exhaustive search of all likely hiding-places. There will be a door-to-door check on all hotels and boarding-houses in Cheltenham itself and the surrounding area; and enquiries are going to be made through local house agents about properties which have been rented out in the last three months. You two are the only people who can actually identify the men we want, so you will co-ordinate the search and check out any possible sightings. Understood?'

'Understood, sir.'

As they rose to leave Nick hesitated.

176

'How is Leonora, sir?'

Pascoe gave him a characteristic look, which suggested that any personal questions about a fellow operative were in poor taste. Then his face softened momentarily. No one knew better than he the spell which both men were under.

'She's well. She's been resting down at her cottage.'

'With someone keeping a discreet eye on her, I hope,' Stone said.

'Oh, very discreet,' Pascoe murmured.

'There's one thing I've been meaning to ask,' Stone said. 'The people who knew her in London—where do they think she's been all this time?'

Pascoe raised his heavy-lidded eyes. 'The employees at the agency think that Laura Cavendish is in New York, setting up an American branch. They get postcards every now and then, speaking of the good progress she's making. And if you had read your gossip columns you'd know that Leonora Carr left England in April for a long stay in a Swiss clinic. Opinion varies as to whether she's drying out, slimming down or simply having a face-lift.'

Stone and Nick exchanged looks.

'What a perfectly ridiculous suggestion!' Nick commented, as they headed for the door.

*   *   *

The painstaking house-to-house search continued for four days but although there were one or two false alarms it did not produce even a hint of Slattery's real whereabouts. On the morning of the fifth day Nick, glancing through the paper over breakfast, exclaimed suddenly,

' 'Allo, 'allo, 'allo! What are they up to now?'

'What's that?' Stone asked, with his mouth full of toast.

Nick passed him the paper. It contained a photograph of a very attractive blonde, arrow-slim in an elegant black dress, descending the steps of an air liner. The caption read 'Lovely Leonora Flies Back to London'.

'Well, I suppose she had to come back sometime,' Stone commented.

'Yes, but why now, I wonder?' Nick murmured.

The answer to his question came over the scrambler from Pascoe about half an hour later.

'I'm sending Omega down to help you,' he said. 'She has a theory that I think might be worth following up. You're to carry on where you are, Stone, and Marriot is to liaise with Omega. You'll find her booked into the Regency Hotel under her usual name. Marriot will be booked in too as chauffeur/secretary. She's expecting you about four.'

Stone put the phone down and looked at

178

Nick.

'Jammy devil!' he said softly.

*　　　*　　　*

Nick showered and shaved with extra care, put on a suit—a rarity for him—and presented himself at the Regency Hotel. The desk clerk gave him a look of scarcely concealed envy and informed him that Miss Carr was in the Jane Austen Suite and was expecting him.

As he knocked on the door his heart was beating as if he had run up the stairs instead of coming up in the lift. He smiled at the voice which answered—low, seductive, beautifully modulated, very different from the harsh tones of Elizabeth Walker. She was sitting in an easy chair by the window, with a magazine on her lap. The cropped hair was concealed by the elegant blond wig which recreated the image of the beautiful star who, with one film, had become the symbol of the ideal, unattainable woman for millions of men. Her make-up was immaculate and the deceptively simple blue dress was cut to flatter her slender body. Only the mischievous grin was the same as ever as she rose and crossed the room to meet him.

'Nick! It's lovely to see you again!'

Her arms were round his neck. He held her close.

'Not half as lovely as it is to see you—looking so marvellous, too.'

He kissed her. She drew her head back and looked at him.

'I'm sorry I had to be such a bitch to you the last few times we met—especially that business in Liverpool. I know what you must have been through.'

'Yes, well . . .' he murmured. 'Let's not talk about that.'

He kissed her again, and this time she responded wholeheartedly.

'Come and sit down,' she said, leading him to a settee.

'You look fantastic!' he marvelled. 'What have you been doing this last week?'

'Not a lot!' she said, with a laugh. 'Lying in the sun—going for long rides on Dippy. In fact, it was that that gave me the idea.'

'What idea?' he asked.

'About where to look for Slattery.' She settled back into the corner of the settee and became practical. He wished he'd somehow asked a different question. 'Would you like some tea?' Leo offered, reaching for the phone.

'Let me,' he said. 'As chauffeur/secretary that would be part of my duties, wouldn't it?'

He called room service and ordered tea.

'Well?' he asked, sitting back.

'Well,' she echoed, 'I started wondering about the horse—the one they brought over from Ireland—and Slattery's code-name, the Horseman. So I rang Control and got them to

180

check out his background. He's always been associated with horses. He was an apprentice jockey at a stable in Newmarket for some time, until he got involved with a shady betting syndicate and got the push. After that he worked as a groom or a stable-lad all over the place. Then, about six months ago, he suddenly came into some money, nobody quite knows from where, and went back to Ireland where he set himself up as a dealer, buying horses over there and shipping them to England for resale.'

'An ideal cover for an IRA man wanting to pass backwards and forwards between the two countries,' Nick commented.

'And not only for him,' Leo agreed. 'I got the impression when they were working me over in, that horse-box that they had some way of concealing a person, or a body, in it. I suspect it has been fitted with a secret compartment, somewhere. But the more I thought about it, the more it seemed that there must be more to it than just a way of getting into the country without raising suspicions. Why did Reilly and Connor take a horse-box trailer with them to Beeston? Presumably they intended to take not only Slattery but the horse back with them—or *a* horse.'

'What would they want with a horse?' Nick asked.

Leo shrugged. 'Search me. Cover again, perhaps. Anyway, the point is if they *are* using

Slattery's horse-dealing business as a cover for something else, they must be living in a place where there is some form of stabling.'

'You're assuming that they've all met up now, I take it,' Nick said.

'Reilly told Connor to tell Slattery to meet them "at the next rendezvous". I'm sure that must be some place around here that they've set up as a safe house.'

'So we start looking for houses with stables,' Nick concluded.

'I think I've got a better idea,' Leo told him. 'This area is thick with stud farms and training stables—not only racing stables, but people training show-jumpers and eventers. A lot of them are what used to be called "landed gentry" who've gone into it to preserve the ancestral acres. They're the sort of people who still come up to London for "the season" and I've met them at dinner parties and night-clubs etc. I got quite friendly with some of them and when they found out I was a keen horsewoman one or two of them invited me down for long weekends. There are two couples particularly, living not far from here, who are really at the centre of everything that goes on in the horse world in this part of the country. If Reilly has set up as a dealer or bought a stable they're bound to have come across him.'

'But you can hardly go and call on them, as Leonora Carr, and say, "Oh, by the way, I'm looking for a suspected IRA terrorist. Have you come across a small, fair Irish horse dealer lately?" Nick objected.

Leo laughed. 'No, I thought we'd be a bit more subtle than that. I decided I'd tell them that I'm thinking of backing a new film, but it's a story about a horse and unless we can find exactly the right animal the whole thing's off. That ought to give us a good excuse for nosing around any stables.'

'What's the film?' Nick asked, amused.

'Would you believe a version of the legend of Perseus and Andromeda? We're looking for a big, grey horse to play Pegasus. You know—the flying horse.'

'You've got to be joking!'

'I don't see why. It's been done before.'

'Anyway, why a grey horse? I thought you'd want a white one.'

'Ignoramus!' She prodded him with a finger tip. 'No one who knows about horses ever refers to them as white, even when they are. They're always known as grey.' She grinned at him 'You'd better keep quiet and let me do the talking. Still,' she added philosophically, 'I could have been worse off with Stone. He probably thinks a fetlock is some kind of judo hold.'

After tea Leo phoned her friends and made appointments to call on them the following morning. Then they spent some time going through lists of stud farms and riding-schools which Leo had brought with her, and working out an itinerary in case they drew a blank there. They had dinner in the hotel and afterwards Leo suggested that they should have coffee and brandy sent up to her suite. As they settled on the sofa again Nick murmured,

'You know, I haven't checked into my room yet. I don't know where they've put me, even.'

Leo curled her legs up and settled into the crook of his arm.

'Your room's through there,' she said, nodding at a connecting door. 'But I can't think why you're bothered about it . . .'

*   *   *

They set off early the next morning, Leo now dressed in beautifully cut jeans and a silk shirt, managing to combine glamour with casual elegance. Their first appointment took them to a lovely Georgian manor-house where their host and hostess greeted Leo with cries of delight and Nick with an amused tolerance which was only just the right side of condescension. They were shown round the stables, but the owners had to admit, with reget, that they had nothing suitable for Leo's purpose. Over coffee Leo remarked,

'By the way, someone told me that there's an Irish chap somewhere in this area who's importing some very good horses from the Republic. I thought I might try him. Do you happen to know where he hangs out?'

Their hosts looked puzzled. They knew of no one who fitted that description. Leo and Nick took their leave and headed for their next appointment.

Here they had to wait while the young man who owned the farm tried out a new horse over some jumps. Leaning on the fence of the paddock Leo watched with a practised eye.

'Useful animal,' she commented.

Nick looked at her. 'Haven't you ever wanted to get involved with this sort of thing yourself?'

'Show-jumping?' She shook her head. 'No, it's too limited—and not good for the horses in the long run. I wouldn't mind having a go at eventing, though.'

'Eventing?'

'Three-day event. Dressage on the first day, to prove that the horse is supple and well-balanced and absolutely obedient to the slightest movement of the rider. Second day—cross-country; a long course over very big jumps. Takes a horse with a lot of scope and courage. Then on the third day show-jumping, to prove that the animal isn't completely knackered after the cross-country.'

'Oh yes, got you,' Nick assented. 'I've seen it on the box. Have you ever tried it?'

'Once or twice, at a fairly elementary level. Dippy isn't really good enough for the big time, and even if he was I haven't got the time to get us both into proper training. It's

185

exciting, though, specially the cross-country.'

'From what I saw it looks bloody dangerous,' Nick said.

She grinned at him. 'Look. You drive fast cars for fun. Stone jumps out of aeroplanes. What's the difference?'

The rider cleared the last fence and cantered over to them.

'Sorry to keep you waiting,' he said as he handed the reins to a girl groom. 'What can I do for you?'

Once again Leo explained what they were looking for, and once again there was nothing suitable in the stable. Over sherry Leo introduced the subject of the Irish dealer; and once again they drew a blank.

The young man suggested they should try some friends of his. Here they were given lunch, but nothing in the way of useful information except a further recommendation to a lady who had a reputation for buying and selling a wide variety of horses.

This was a very much less aristocratic-looking establishment and they found the owner in the middle of mucking out a loose-box.

'Isn't that funny!' she exclaimed, when Leo had finished explaining what they wanted. 'You're the second lot this week looking for a big grey horse—only the first ones wanted one that could jump not fly!'

Nick sensed that Leo had suddenly become

186

alert—had she been a horse herself her ears would have pricked up.

'It wasn't a big, dark man with an American accent, was it?' she asked. 'I've heard there's an American company after the same screenplay.'

'Oh no,' the woman reassured her. 'This was a little fair chap—Irish by the sound of him.'

'Did you sell him a horse?' Leo asked.

'Wish I could have done! Unfortunately the only grey in the stables at the moment is a little Welsh pony mare. No, I sent him over to old Jake Fairbairn at Combe Martin. He had a super grey last time I was there—terrific jumper, too.'

'Could you give us the address?' Leo asked. 'He might not have sold it.'

Jake Fairbairn was a small man with a skin like leather who had obviously lived and breathed horses since the day he was born.

'The grey?' he said. 'Sorry, my dear, I sold him just the other day. Chap looking for a horse to send out to Ireland to train for eventing. Mind you, I told him, that horse was really too old for what he wanted. Fine animal, terrific jump in him, but a bit of a devil when he wants to be. Too late to start training him for all the fancy stuff. I tried to persuade him to take that bay gelding over there, but no. He said it had got to be a grey. Apparently it's for some old girl who's got some kind of superstition about grey horses being lucky.'

'Do you have his address?' Leo asked. 'Perhaps we could buy the horse off him, if it's still in the country.'

Jake obligingly looked out all the paperwork for them. The cheque was signed by Slattery, but the only address was that of his farm in Cork. They thanked the old man and returned to the car.

'Well,' Nick said, 'at least we know that Slattery was here four days ago.'

'Buying a grey horse . . .' Leo murmured. 'Didn't you say the one he brought over from Ireland was a big grey, too?'

'So it was, now you mention it,' Nick agreed. 'It begins to look as if he and Reilly wanted that horse for some reason, and when it had to be left behind at Beeston they had to go looking for a substitute.'

'But why do they want a big grey horse?' Leo asked.

'As a ringer—a substitute, perhaps? You don't think they're planning another Shergar-type job? Intending to snatch a valuable horse to hold to ransom, and leave the ringer in its place to delay the discovery and give them time to get it out of the country.'

'It's a thought,' Leo agreed, 'although I can't think offhand of a really famous grey horse—nothing with the impact of Shergar.'

They brooded on the problem in silence for a while. Then Nick said,

'I suggest we go and chat it over with Stone.

188

He may have some ideas.'

'Well, we're not going to do any more good out here,' Leo agreed.

They had driven for a couple of miles when they passed a cottage with small white tables set out in the garden under bright sun umbrellas. A notice outside advertised 'Cream Teas.'

'Oh, let's stop for tea, Nick,' Leo exclaimed. 'I haven't had tea in a place like that since I was a kid!'

They parked the car and settled themselves at a table. Leo tilted her face to the sun.

'This is nice. Do you know, it's only been in this last week that I've realized it's summer? It was April when I went undercover in that awful back street in Liverpool, and ever since then I seem to have been cooped up in one stuffy little room after another—except for that expedition to Wales, which was hardly a picnic!'

Nick ordered tea, and while they waited for it Leo began turning over the pages of a copy of *Horse and Hound* which she had brought from the car.

'Geronimo!' The exclamation, coming from such an elegant and sophisticated source, turned the heads of several people at nearby tables.

'What?' Nick asked.

Leo was staring at the magazine, wide-eyed. After a moment, she pursed her lips in a soundless whistle, folded back the page and passed it to him.

'I hope you can swim, sunshine—because I think we're in out of our depth!'

Nick looked at the page in question. It was largely taken up by a photograph of a young woman in impeccable riding gear, mounted on a large grey horse. The caption underneath read,

'HRH Princess Anne, Mrs Mark Phillips, on her grey gelding Fidelio, which she will be riding in the 3-day Event Olympic Trial at Gatcombe Park this week.'

'What day is it?' Leo demanded.

'Friday,' Nick told her.

'Dressage today; cross-country tomorrow,' Leo said. 'And Slattery wanted a horse that could jump . . .'

CHAPTER NINE

Stone, Nick and Leo were waiting for Pascoe in the hotel room where he had set up his HQ. He came in briskly and settled himself behind the desk.

'Well,' he said, 'It's on. There was a lot of opposition from various sources, but I managed to persuade them in the end.'

There was a stir in the room, a movement compounded of excitement and apprehension. All three men looked at Leo.

Pascoe said, 'I hope you can handle this, Leonora. I don't mean the Slattery end of it— that's part of the job and anyway you'll have the whole of Triple S to back you up—I mean the rest of it.'

Leo gave him a small, ironic smile. 'I guess it's something I've always wanted to have a go at. Now's my chance.'

*   *   *

Gatcombe Park was thronged with people— competitors and their friends; horse-boxes carrying some of the finest horses in the world with their attendant grooms; and spectators, some of them *aficionados* who followed such events from Burghley to Badminton and now to this new course at Gatcombe, others who had simply seized the opportunity to get a closer look at a royal residence. The crowds were much larger than for the dressage competition the day before and those who noticed an increased police presence and tighter security probably put it down to this fact. For most people it was just a minor annoyance that they were kept too far back from the course to get a really close look at the competitors.

On the crest of some rising ground which

gave the most comprehensive view of the course available, Nick stood by a police Range Rover and studied the landscape around him intently through powerful field-glasses. The cross-country course stretched for several miles through the undulating parkland of the estate and it was impossible for anyone to see all of it at once; but the sections which were out of his sight were covered by other Triple S operatives and periodically Nick put down his glasses in order to check with each of them by radio. The competition was already under way, the riders setting off at two-minute intervals, and the leaders were now about half-way round the course. So far there had been no sign of Slattery or Reilly and the rest, and nothing to give rise to any suspicion.

Above Nick's head, so high that the clamour of its rotor blades was hardly more than a whisper, a helicopter hung in the air while Stone, sitting beside the pilot, also swept the ground with his glasses, paying particular attention to any activity along the roads which bordered the estate. The whole situation was a security nightmare; miles of open countryside, and a constant flow of people and vehicles in and out of the gates.

A louder cheer than usual from the crowd around the start drew Nick's attention. He turned his glasses on the spot and his lips tightened in a small, grim smile as he saw the big grey horse carrying the royal colours canter out onto the course.

Leo eased her weight forward over the horse's shoulders and relaxed her hands fractionally on the reins, and felt his stride lengthen as he settled into a steady gallop. The first hurdle, metaphorically speaking, was behind her. Under the jockey silks and the peaked helmet with its broad chin strap no one had spotted the substitution. Now she could concentrate on the course itself. Her mouth was dry, but it was not because she was worrying about what Slattery might be planning. Stone and Nick could take care of him. All that mattered to her, at that moment, was getting herself and the horse round the course without damage to either of them— quite apart from the fact that if she fell off too soon her imposture would be revealed and the whole scheme would collapse. She had walked the course that morning with Pascoe and the other two, in the early dawn light after the bomb disposal boys had finished their sweep; and the size of some of the jumps, seen close to, had made the palms of her hands sweat.

The first obstacle was approaching—a nice, straightforward post and rails built round a folly in the grounds of the house; big, but not treacherous. She saw Fidelio's ears go forward and his stride lengthened again. She dropped her weight back into the saddle and tightened the reins until his speed slackened and his body bunched so that the impulsion imparted by the powerful hindquarters was converted into upwards motion. Two strides away from the fence she let him have his head and they soared up and over the obstacle as if the horse had suddenly sprouted wings. Leo caught her breath at the sheer sense of power. Her own horse, Serendipity, was more than adequate for most purposes, but this was like getting out of a family saloon and into a Lamborghini.

Fidelio was already cantering on strongly towards the next fence and, reassured by his capacity, she was able to think for a moment about the real object of the exercise. If she was right, Slattery intended at some point to substitute the horse he had bought for Fidelio; but perhaps her assumption that he also intended some hostile act against his rider was mistaken. Maybe all he planned to do was to steal the horse out of its stable during the night. If so, she reflected grimly, and the imposture which she had undertaken turned out to be unnecessary, she would be extremely unpopular in several quarters. On the other hand . . . she thought for a moment how easy it would be to hide a bomb in a drain or under a bush and explode it by remote control; but then, why would he need a substitute horse?

They were approaching the next jump, a big wall of Gloucestershire stone. Confident now in Fidelio's ability she let him have his head. As a result he ran at the wall, flattened over the top of it and caught a hind foot on the farther edge. The touch unbalanced him so that he stumbled on landing, pitching Leo forward and to one side so that she was hanging alongside his neck. The horse recovered immediately and galloped on, but for a few frantic moments Leo found herself watching the ground as it hurtled past beneath her while nothing but her own will-power, it seemed, kept her attached to the saddle. Finally she managed to haul herself upright and regain her stirrups, resolving as she did so that from now on she would concentrate entirely on riding.

In the helicopter Stone swept the course ahead of her for the hundredth time, checked, went back, refocused his glasses and shouted to the pilot.

'Take us down a couple of hundred feet. I think I may have spotted something.'

As the machine dropped Stone concentrated on a patch of woodland which clothed the sides of a small valley. Then he lowered his glasses and reached for the radio microphone.

'Delta One to Kappa Two. Come in please.'

There was no reply. He called again.

'Kappa Two, this is Delta One. Do you read me?'

Still there was silence from the speaker in his headset.

Stone tried again.

'Delta Two, this is Delta One. Come in

please.'

Nick answered at once. 'Delta Two here. Go ahead.'

'I think I've spotted a vehicle of some sort in the small copse in the north-eastern quarter. I've tried to call Viv, but I can't raise him. I estimate Omega is within two minutes of that point. Can you investigate?'

'I'm on my way. Delta Two out.'

Nick was already moving towards the Range Rover and within seconds it was heading down the hill in the direction of the valley.

Fidelio crested a rise and strode on down the slope. They were past the half-way mark now but he was still full of going. Leo blinked ahead of her. Some of the worst jumps were behind her but there were still plenty to come. The muscles in her back and shoulders were screaming with the strain of balancing herself and controlling the big horse's raking stride, and her thighs had turned to jelly. Her only thought now was to stay with him until the end of the course. 'And I thought I was fit!' she commented inwardly.

As she looked towards the copse of trees her eye was caught by a sudden glint of light. She searched the spot and saw it again and instantly knew what it was. The sun, which was behind her, was being reflected off the lenses of a pair of binoculars—or the telescopic sight on a rifle. She forgot her aching muscles. Someone there at the edge of the wood was watching her progress. It might be an innocent spectator, of course, but why should anyone choose to watch the event from there, where there was no obstacle to jump? She became aware of a noise and looked up. Stone's helicopter was dropping steadily out of the sky towards the trees.

As she entered the wood the sudden change from brilliant sunlight to deep shade unsighted her for a moment. She tried to check Fidelio's speed, but the big grey was homewards bound and pulling like a train. Then she saw it, twenty yards ahead of them, a rope stretched tight from tree to tree across the path, about eighteen inches from the ground, a certain trap for a horse and rider expecting no such hazard. Leo flung her weight back in the saddle and hauled on the reins, only to feel the grey set his jaw and gallop on. All she could do was drag his head round and aim him for the trees. As they crashed into the undergrowth at the edge of the path a figure rose from a crouching position and leapt for the horse's head. Fidelio shied violently and Leo slipped her left foot out of the stirrup and kicked out as hard as she could. She felt her toe connect with the man's jaw and in the same instant recognized Patrick Connor. It was only a glancing blow, but with Fidelio's mass and speed behind it it was enough to send him staggering backwards over a fallen branch. The horse crashed on, weaving between the trees and it was then that Leo saw her double—a big grey horse, identical at a superficial glance to Fidelio, mounted by a slight figure in the royal colours. In a moment of revelation she saw why the fair, slim-built Slattery was so essential to the plot.

Slattery's horse was already giving him trouble, backing and jerking his head against the restraining bit, but when Fidelio hurtled out of the trees into the clearing where they were waiting he lost control completely. The horse leaped forward, yanking the reins through his fingers, and bolted away down the track. Leo was aware of other figures running and shouting among the trees and of a sudden shattering roar as the helicopter appeared at tree-top level; but her main concern now was to catch up with Slattery. For the first time she really let Fidelio stretch himself and they pounded down the track after the impostor.

At the bottom of the valley was a small stream and in the middle of this, where the path crossed it, a fence had been built so that each rider had the choice of either descending a steep bank, jumping into the stream and scrambling out up an equally steep bank on the far side, or of making a single leap from the top of one bank to the other. Slattery's horse saw the jump too late, attempted to stop, skidded down the bank, took off in a desperate bid to clear the fence, caught its forefeet on the top rail and somersaulted into the stream, flinging Slattery out of the saddle to land with a stunning thud on the far bank. Leo, close behind, had only time to set the big grey back on his hocks and prevent him too from sliding head first down the slope. She felt him gather himself for a great leap and as he took off the other horse struggled to its feet and made off down the bed of the stream, leaving Slattery still sprawled on the opposite side. Fidelio cleared the stream and the fence with inches to spare but to ask him to clear Slattery's body as well was too much. Even so, he might have succeeded if the Irishman had not tried to struggle to his feet. The horse's front hoofs struck the ground just beyond him but as he raised his head one of the powerful hind feet crashed down on his jaw and he dropped back without a sound.

They were half-way up the opposite slope before Leo was able to bring the horse to a standstill and look back. Slattery lay where he had fallen and from the angle of his neck it was obvious that he was dead. For a moment Leo sat still, feeling the horse's flanks heaving beneath her. Somewhere nearby she could hear the helicopter, very low. She remembered the running figures among the trees and turned to canter on up the hill to clearer ground, where she could get a better view of the situation.

*   *   *

The Range Rover was still several hundred yards from the trees when Stone's voice crackled over the radio.

'There's something happening down there. I can see people running. Watch out! There's a truck or something heading your way.'

An instant later a horse-box appeared from the cover of the trees, its tail-board still lowered and bouncing along the ground and roared away at top speed along a narrow farm track.

'After them!' Nick shouted to his driver, and the Range Rover swung to the right, bouncing over the uneven pasture land. A figure crouched in the back of it. It was Margaret Donelly.

As they began to overhaul the box Nick became aware of her and she had a rifle—at her shoulder. At the same moment a bullet clanged into the roof of the Range Rover and ricocheted off. Nick drew his automatic. Seated as he was beside the driver the window was on his left and he knew that, with the two vehicles bumping and swaying as they were, he had no hope of finding his target with a left-handed shot. He wound down the window and eased the top half of his body through it, bracing himself with one foot against the dashboard. As he did so a second bullet sang past his head, actually nicking the top of his ear. He grasped the gun in both hands and took aim, intending a disabling shot to the shoulder. He squeezed the trigger and saw Donelly jerk upwards and drop the rifle. Then she toppled forwards and at the same moment the horse-box bounced violently, pitching her headfirst onto the ground, where she lay without moving.

The Range Rover drew level with the box and Nick could see Reilly in the driver's seat, an expression of wild determination on his thin face. He levelled his automatic and yelled,

'Pack it in, Reilly! It's all over.'

For answer Reilly twisted the steering-wheel so that the van veered sharply towards the police car, forcing the driver to brake violently, almost throwing Nick out. As he regained his balance he took aim again, this time at the front off-side wheel, and saw the tyre explode. The horse-box swerved, tilted on the slope of the field and looked for a moment as if it was going to turn over. As it came to a standstill Reilly leaped out, a rifle in his hand, and ran round to take cover behind it. Nick's driver skidded round the front of it and as he did so Reilly's bullet shattered the window just behind him.

'Get down!' Nick shouted, as the car came to a halt, and they both piled out on the far side and took cover.

Nick looked around him. Over the hill which hid them from the house a small convoy of vehicles was approaching, led by another police Range Rover. Nick guessed that Pascoe had picked up the radio traffic at his command post and was coming to investigate. Reilly saw them too and made a last bid to escape. Leaping to his feet he started running like a stag towards the wall which bounded the estate. Nick followed but the Irishman turned and fired a shot which ripped through the cloth of Nick's trousers and left a long graze along his thigh. Nick swore and ran on, feeling the warm blood trickling down his leg; but as Reilly turned again for another shot there was a sudden deafening roar and the helicopter appeared over a band of trees and dropped to within a few feet of the ground right in his path. Reilly tried to swerve away to his right, but the chopper slid sideways and again intercepted him. Nick heard Stone's voice over the loud hailer.

'Give yourself up, Reilly. You're surrounded. You haven't got a prayer.'

For a moment Reilly glared wildly around him, from the helicopter to Nick, now lying full length with his automatic braced in both hands and levelled at Reilly's chest, and beyond him to the approaching convoy of cars. Then he dropped his gun and raised his hands.

By the time Nick had handcuffed him and handed him over to his police driver for safe keeping the helicopter had set Stone down. Nick walked over to join him. Stone nodded at the rip in his trouser leg.

'Another couple of inches and that could have been very unfortunate,' he remarked dryly.

'Any sign of the rest of them?' Nick asked.

Stone jerked his head towards the chopper. 'Both the Connors are in there. They came out of the wood on the far side like a couple of rabbits. All I had to do was pick them up.'

'What about Leo?'

'Haven't you seen her?'

Nick shook his head.

Stone said, 'I saw her go into the trees. In fact, I thought I saw two horses in there, but I don't know what happened to them. I haven't seen Slattery or Donelly either.'

Nick pointed back along the track to where a dark shape still lay on the grass.

'Donelly's over there.'

They started to walk back towards the place and as they did so a riderless grey horse cantered out of the trees in the bed of the valley and headed off over the hill. The two men stared after it.

'That's her horse!' Nick said.

'Could be,' Stone replied, 'but I told you, I saw two horses in there—both white, and both the riders were wearing the same colours. My guess is one of them could be Slattery.'

At that moment a second horse appeared at the top of the hill, paused for a second and then cantered towards them. They both strained their eyes to recognize the rider but under the peaked helmet it was impossible. Acting on the same instinct they both drew their guns. The rider halted a few yards off.

'Hey!' Leo shouted. 'Do you mind? I'm on your side, remember?'

Laughing with relief they ran towards her. She swung her leg across the saddle and dismounted, but as her feet touched the ground her knees buckled and she would have fallen if Stone had not caught hold of her.

'What is it?' he asked anxiously.

She shook her head, half laughing. 'It's all right. My legs have gone to jelly, that's all. I had no idea that this sort of ride was such hard work!'

She hung onto him for a moment and then straightened up.

'Have you seen Reilly and the others?'

'Reilly and the Connors are in the bag,' Stone told her. 'Do you know what's happened to Slattery?'

She nodded towards the wood. 'He's back there—dead, I'm afraid. His horse threw him, and then this fellow here jumped on top of him. There was nothing I could do about it.'

Stone gave her shoulders a comforting squeeze.

'I wouldn't let it worry you too much. According to our records he was probably involved in the Hyde Park bombing—so there's a kind of poetic justice about it.'

'What about Margaret?' Leo asked.

Stone and Nick exchanged looks. Nick said, 'She's over there. She was firing at us from the back of the horse-box. I had to take her out. I aimed for a disabling shot, but with both the vehicles bouncing about so much it was tricky.'

They walked on towards the prone figure. Nick reached her first and was shocked to discover that her eyes were open and she was not only still alive but conscious, although she lay without moving as he approached. Her body was twisted at an awkward angle and he instinctively knelt to straighten it out.

'Don't touch her,' Leo said tonelessly from behind him. 'It looks as if her neck's broken. If you try to move her you could kill her. Leave her to the ambulance men.' Nick looked up at her, feeling suddenly sick. Leo went on, 'It wasn't your shot. Look, that hit her in the arm, as you intended. She must have fallen on her head coming out of the box.'

Margaret had recognized the voice and her eyes had been searching for the source of it. Now they found Leo. Leo reached up and undid the chin-strap of her riding helmet, pulling it off to reveal her short hair stuck close to her scalp with sweat. She moved quietly to where the other girl could see her without difficulty.

'Yes, I'm afraid so, Margaret,' she said, replying to the unspoken question. 'Reilly was quite right. You should never have trusted me.

But then, you should never have shot that copper in Liverpool—or helped to organize those car bombs in Belfast that you boasted to me about.'

The two women looked at each other in silence for a moment, and then Leo turned and walked away a short distance, to stand with her back to them and her head bowed. Once again Nick and Stone consulted each other's eyes. In the end it was Nick who turned to where Fidelio, who had forgotten he was in a race, was quietly cropping the grass; leaving Stone to go over to Leo and put an arm around her shoulders.

*   *   *

That evening the three of them and Pascoe dined privately in Leo's hotel suite. Leo, showered and rested but still with a look of porcelain fragility about her, reclined on a couch dressed in a white and gold silk caftan which belonged to her Leonora Carr wardrobe. Pascoe, half-way down a pre-prandial gin and tonic, was tying off the loose threads in their day's work.

'We checked out the horse-box. It belongs to Slattery, part of his legitimate business, like the one that was left behind at Beeston and it came over three days ago via Swansea with a horse which was sold, again quite legitimately, in the Bristol area. You were quite right, Leo,

206

there is a secret compartment built into the bulkhead between the cabin and the horse-box itself, with just enough room for one person to lie down. We also found a hypodermic syringe and several ampoules of a powerful sedative.'

'So they planned to bring the horse down, grab the rider, dope her and hide her in the secret compartment,' Leo murmured. 'But did they really think they'd get her out of the country?'

'Not immediately, I think,' Pascoe replied. 'The van is booked to return to Cork tonight but I found it hard to believe that they would actually take that risk. That was where the forensic boys came up with the goods. They found some feathers caught in the hinge of the tail-board which they were able to identify as turkey feathers. We ran a check on all turkey farmers in the area, and found one just six miles from Gatcombe. Analysis of the soil in the treads of the tyres agreed with the type of soil found around there, so we decided to check it out.'

'Just a minute,' Leo said, 'I thought you two had already investigated all the farms and places where Slattery might be lying low.'

'We were looking at properties which had changed hands or been let within the last few months,' Stone said. 'This one hadn't.'

'The owner is—was—a respected member of the local community,' Pascoe continued. 'He had owned the farm for four years and was running a prosperous business. He was known as a keen horseman who regularly rode to hounds during the season. No one had any idea that he had the remotest connection with Ireland—until we looked into his background.'

'A sleeper!' Leo said.

'Quite so,' Pascoe agreed.

'So that was where Slattery and Co. had been hiding,' Leo said, 'but do you mean they intended to take HRH back there?'

'We've got proof that they did,' Stone told her. 'We practically had to take the place apart, brick by brick, to get it—but there's no doubt. There's a cellar under the farmhouse. They'd built a wall partitioning off one end— very cleverly done; at first sight you'd think it had been there since the house was built. The door was hidden behind some shelves full of old paint cans and such. Inside there was a little room with a bed and a bucket—basic but adequate. Anyone could have been kept shut away in there almost indefinitely and we'd never have known where to look without the evidence of the van.'

'And the van would have been on its way back to Ireland,' Leo said.

'And if it had been stopped and searched— as it would have been under the circumstances—they would simply have been going about their legitimate business. They still had all the papers connected with the purchase of the horse from Fairbairn. No one would have spotted that it was a different animal; and they would have been taking it back to Ireland for their client exactly as they told Fairburn they intended to do.'

'Suppose they'd been stopped leaving the grounds?' Leo said. 'They couldn't have used that story then.'

'No,' Pascoe agreed, 'in that case they would have been a competitor retiring early because of injury or a similar reason. We found all the necessary documentation for that in the van, too. Besides, that was where Slattery came in. His job was to complete the course so that no one realized that anything was wrong. As you saw, the horses were almost identical and the rider hard to recognize at a distance. It would have taken him at least another ten or fifteen minutes to reach the finish. By that time the horse-box would have been back at the farm—and the prisoner transferred to her specially built cell.'

'And what was supposed to happen to Slattery? He couldn't have hoped to escape.'

Pascoe nodded. 'That's true. There would appear to be an element of kamikaze about Slattery's mission. But not so much as you might think. One thing we have managed to learn from Liam Connor is the object of the exercise. They planned to demand the release of all IRA and INLA prisoners in jail in both England and Northern Ireland. The main idea was to get back all the top brass they lost owing to the "supergrass" trials, but presumably Slattery would have benefitted from the amnesty too.'

There was a silence. At length Nick said, 'You know, it could have worked.'

Pascoe's face was grave. 'It came much too near to working for my peace of mind,' he said. 'If it hadn't been for you, Leo . . . and you two . . .'

Leo grinned suddenly. 'It wouldn't have worked, you know. Slattery didn't have a chance of finishing the course on that animal. It may have looked a dead ringer, but in terms of actual performance it hadn't got a hope. After all Slattery's experience—fancy letting old Jake Fairbairn put one over on him like that!'

They all laughed, the sudden laughter of relief after prolonged strain. Then Leo said, 'Incidentally, has it occurred to anyone how curious it is that the horse should be called Fidelio?'

They looked at her, puzzled.

'No,' Nick said, 'why?'

Pascoe chuckled abruptly. 'Yes, of course! How odd!'

Nick and Stone exchanged looks and shook their heads.

'Oh, come on, Nick,' Leo teased him, 'Stone may be a musical illiterate, but you're not. Think! Fidelio . . .'

He frowned, concentrating. 'Opera—by

210

Beethoven.'

'Good! And the name of the heroine?'

'Oh, got you! Leonora!'

'Who,' concluded Pascoe, 'in the course of the plot, disguises herself in order to get into the prison where her husband is incarcerated.'

'I'd forgotten that,' Nick said. 'You're right. It is a strange coincidence.'

Stone cleared his throat, finished his Scotch and leaned back in his chair. The conversation, he felt, was getting onto altogether the wrong lines.

'Anyway,' he said, 'I reckon that ought to be worth a medal apiece, don't you?'

'I wouldn't count on it,' Pascoe told him drily. 'I understand she wants to know who the bloody fool was in the helicopter who frightened all the horses!'